WONDER WOMAN™
at SUPER HERO HIGH

By Lisa Yee

Random House 🏠 New York

To Jodi Reamer, an original Super Hero Girl

All rights reserved. Published in the United States by Random House Children's
Books, a division of Penguin Random House LLC, 1745 Broadway, New York, NY
10019, and in Canada by Penguin Random House Canada Limited, Toronto. Random
House and the colophon are registered trademarks of Penguin Random House LLC.
randomhousekids.com
dcsuperherogirls.com
ISBN 978-1-101-94059-4 (hc) — ISBN 978-1-101-94060-0 (lib. bdg.)
ISBN 978-1-101-94061-7 (ebook)
Printed in the United States of America
10 9 8 7 6 5 4 3 2 1

PROLOGUE

It was barely the third week of school, and already someone had been expelled. The rumors were flying so fast that if you weren't careful, you could get whiplash from trying to follow the speeding gossip. But when anyone asked Principal Amanda "The Wall" Waller about it, she'd cross her strong arms, arch an eyebrow, and say in her booming *how-dare-you* voice, "You weren't talking to *me*, were you?"

Never had a question elicited so much silence. The super heroes-in-training at Super Hero High weren't brave enough—or dumb enough—to ask a second time.

The buzz was big. Even the most studious Supers were finding it hard to focus. In Weaponomics class, Mr. Fox had to resort to stink-bombing the room to get everyone's attention. If it had been light-fingered Catwoman or chilly Frost or even boisterous Cyborg who had been expelled, you probably would have heard things like . . .

"Yeah, I knew that would happen."

"Why did it take so long?"

"Really? Wow. Now tell me something I didn't know."

But quiet and unassuming Mandy Bowin?

Instead, the most frequently asked question was "Mandy *who*?"

As a transfer student, Mandy had the audacity to be fairly normal in a school of abnormally competitive high achievers. Without superpowers, a superior IQ, or—much more important—a strong personality, it was a miracle she'd been accepted in the first place. Or maybe, according to some rumors, her acceptance had been a mistake. That made more sense. Naturally, thoughts of Mandy Bowin vanished as quickly as *she* had. Besides, there was a fresh new rumor to obsess over—not so much *who* had been banished, but the reason *why* behind the reason why.

Cheetah had come up with the theory, and it quickly spread thanks to Harley Quinn's penchant for gossip, fueled in no small part by HQTV, her new self-produced "All Harley all the time!" video channel.

"It wasn't that The Wall wanted Mandy out," Cheetah purred to the camera, "but that she wanted a certain someone *in*. And with enrollment at an all-time high, well, *au revoir*, Mandy!"

As with many Internet rumors, it didn't matter if Cheetah's theory had any basis in reality . . . instantly, people began repeating it as gospel, even though most students knew there was no enrollment limit at Super Hero High. So—was it true, or was Cheetah just bored again and trying to scare up mischief? She was famous for her schemes. Like the time she rigged a fake Save the Day alarm just so she could get out of taking a super hero history test.

Most students were in the process of becoming whichever super hero they were destined to be. They still hadn't fully mastered their superpowers, and some were not quite as courageous as they would be down the road. And unfortunately, a few might have even lacked much of a conscience. But no one was without an opinion.

According to Cheetah, there was only one person Principal Waller would forego the normal admissions channels for. Tales of this teen warrior princess's exploits were legendary. She was, as Bumblebee overheard The Wall saying, a "one-of-a-kind catch." Every school on Earth—and even a few on other planets—wanted her.

Which brings us back to the expulsion. When Mandy Bowin was forcibly removed, she was heard yelling at Principal Waller, "I'll be back!"

It was hard to tell if that was a promise or a threat. And even more interesting was that if Cheetah was right, Super Hero High was about to be turned upside down.

PART ONE

CHAPTER 1

Wonder Woman sat with her mouth hanging open. She knew it was unbecoming of a warrior princess and heir to the Amazon throne, but her mind was on other things—specifically, the video streaming on her computer. Without telling her mother, she had sent away for the secret code to access it, and had also emailed a letter that read in part:

Dear Principal Amanda Waller,
My name is Wonder Woman, and I am interested in
attending the prestigious Super Hero High School.
Having been homeschooled all my life here on Paradise
Island, I don't have the required transcripts. However,
I am athletic, courageous, and willing to do whatever it
takes to make the world a better place.

As Wonder Woman watched the Super Hero High recruitment video, she was interrupted by an urgent message flashing on her computer screen.

HIGH ALERT: CALLING ALL SUPER HEROES IN THE VICINITY OF THE BERMUDA TRIANGLE! AN AMERICAN TOUR BOAT CARRYING SECOND GRADERS ON A FIELD TRIP IS IN THE PATH OF A MONSTER TIDAL WAVE. . . .

Wonder Woman didn't need to hear anything more before hitting Pause, grabbing her unbreakable Lasso of Truth, and racing out of her room.

Her mother was rearranging boulders in the garden again. "Where are you going?" she asked.

"To save second grade," Wonder Woman explained, already in flight.

"Be home by dinner!" her mom called after her.

The first to arrive at the scene, Wonder Woman could hear children screaming as the mountain of water arched menacingly above them. Their boat began to rock violently. Instantly, Wonder Woman whipped out her Lasso of Truth. She had only one chance to save the students before the crush of the ocean would capsize their vessel.

Wonder Woman raised her lasso high above her head, and with deft precision, threw it hard. On target! She had ringed the mast. With a flip of her wrist, she yanked on the lasso, tightening the loop, then used the rope to keep the boat upright as the giant wave passed under it. The children cheered.

"Thank you, young lady!" their teacher cried. "You're our hero!"

Wonder Woman blushed and waved before heading home. If she hurried, there was still time to watch the rest of the recruitment video before dinner.

Back home, Wonder Woman leaned forward and studied the video. Super Hero High School was everything she had ever dreamed of. The school boasted an expansive campus with a gleaming high-rise in the center. It offered its students and faculty up-to-the-moment technology, gadgets, and weapons to die for. Plus there was the recently unveiled Flight Track and the much-used on-campus hospital. And the only thing more impressive than the inspirational statue of Justice herself was the iconic Amethyst from Gemworld that sat atop the school's highest tower, piercing the clouds and doubling as a welcoming beacon for incoming flyers.

Oh! And there were classes taught by celebrity super hero alumni, and more clubs than anyone could possibly have time for, like Playing with Poisons, Cooking with Swords, and the ever-popular Knitting and Hitting. But what Wonder Woman found most fascinating were the students.

Every kind of teenager imaginable was represented—some with multiple superpowers, and others with none at all. Many of the snootier schools, like Interstellar Magnet, only considered students based on their grades, test scores, and superpower pedigree. But Super Hero High had a loftier goal. Here, students were selected not based on who they were today, *but on who they could become tomorrow*. Girls, boys, animals, insects, aliens, robots, mutants, morphers—they were all in the video. This was an equal-opportunity school, and it appealed to Wonder Woman's keen sense of justice.

She also noted that the students looked deliriously happy, especially one peppy, pigtailed blond girl who managed to be in almost every scene. As Wonder Woman imagined herself making friends, she felt a warmth wash over her. This wasn't like the time she was knocked over by an atomic fireball. No, this warmth made her smile inside and out.

As the video came to a close, the music swelled and a diverse group of students and teachers stood or hovered behind Principal Waller, who was saying, "So if you want to super-charge your education"—Wonder Woman nodded—"meet super friends"—Wonder Woman nodded—"and make a super difference"—Wonder Woman nodded—"then we welcome you to Super Hero High!"

There was a lump in Wonder Woman's throat. Just as tears were starting to form, she heard the boom of a woman's strong voice.

"Wonder Woman!"

Huh?

Who was calling her?

It was the computer—or, to be more exact, it was Amanda

Waller on the computer. The principal had embedded a personal message at the end of the recruitment video.

Wonder Woman sat up straight and adjusted the small gold tiara that was nestled atop her long, thick black hair. "Yes, ma'am," she said, even though she knew Principal Waller couldn't hear her. Wonder Woman had been raised to be respectful.

The principal attempted a smile. This did not suit her stern face; it made her look like she had indigestion. In the background, Wonder Woman could see the Federal Service Agent of the Year awards lining the walls. She had read dozens of interviews about the head of Super Hero High, and though Amanda Waller had no traditional superpowers of her own, she was credited with keeping injuries to a minimum, scaring the heebie-jeebies out of the students, and always demanding the best from her young super heroes.

"Wonder Woman," Principal Waller said. Her broad shoulders took up the bottom half of the computer screen. "I have had my eyes on you for quite a while, and I feel the time has come for you to join us. You have the potential to become one of the greatest super heroes in history. But you lack formal super hero training. That's where Super Hero High comes in. I want you to think about this, but listen to your heart as well. It knows where you belong."

"*What* are you watching?"

Wonder Woman jerked her head around. "I . . . I was just . . ."

"I can see what you are doing," her mother said, standing tall and looking every bit the warrior queen she was. "Why would you want to leave Paradise Island?"

It was a fair question. Their home was a lush tropical island surrounded by a turquoise sea so blue, it defied definition. Warm water lapped the golden shores, creating white ribbons of waves that made it look as if the island itself were a gift. Maybe it was. Serene rolling hills played host to majestic green trees. Wispy white willows bent gracefully in the wind—but like so many things, they were not what they seemed. Even a chainsaw couldn't make a dent in the most delicate-looking willow, because the island, though a paradise, was also a fortress inhabited solely by Amazon warrior women.

In the heart of Paradise Island—also known as Themyscira—a grand Greek temple rose above the trees. It was here that Hippolyta, Queen of the Amazons, lived with her only daughter.

"It's not that I want to leave." Wonder Woman struggled to explain to her mother. "It's just that I want to go places. I want to make a difference to the entire world."

Hippolyta's silence made her nervous. Her mother was always silent before going into battle. Was this what their conversation would be? A battle? The two had always been close. Wonder Woman hoped she could keep it at the level of debate.

"Please, Mother," Wonder Woman begged. "I can learn so much at Super Hero High. All the greatest super heroes have gone there."

"I didn't go there," Hippolyta noted.

"That's not what I meant," Wonder Woman said quickly. "It's just that, well, I've been here on Paradise Island all my life, and I . . ."

Hippolyta let out a big sigh—the one mothers reserve for their children when they have so much to say but can't get it all out.

"My dearest daughter," she said, her voice softening. "You were born to be a leader. You have royalty in your blood. Stay here, and someday you will rule Paradise Island and be Queen of the Amazons, just like me."

Now it was time for Wonder Woman to be silent. She breathed deeply before saying, "Mother, I love and admire you. But when I grow up, I want to be just like *me.*"

Hippolyta loved her daughter more than anything, and she understood the depth of the desire that Wonder Woman had to explore the outside world. And so she finally agreed to let her daughter go, but not before giving her a gift. "These have served me well for years," Hippolyta said, removing her cuff bracelets. "They will deflect missiles and bullets and other weapons that aim to harm you."

"Thank you, Mother," Wonder Woman said, looking down at the gleaming metal bracelets that now graced her wrists.

She used to try on her mother's cuffs when she was younger, but they were always too big and slid off. Today, however, for the first time, they fit perfectly.

"I will be checking on you, often," Hippolyta said. "You will be our Amazon Ambassador and must behave accordingly."

"I promise," Wonder Woman assured her. She wondered how she could feel pain and happiness at the same time. As much as she would miss her mother and Paradise Island, the only home she had ever known, Wonder Woman was excited about the new life that lay before her.

As if reading her mind, her mother said, "Dearest, you have royal blood and are the princess and heir to this island of Amazon women warriors. But I will not keep you back, for wherever you go, you shall always hold the place of honor in my heart, my beloved daughter."

"Thank you, Mother," Wonder Woman said, wiping tears from her eyes. She wondered if the bracelets really did work. They could not deflect the pain that tugged at her heart.

They embraced, and before her mother could change her mind about letting her go, Wonder Woman was off, flying faster than she had ever flown before. Having never been away from Paradise Island longer than the short time it took to save lives and right wrongs in nearby locations, she savored her newfound feeling of freedom. Marveling at the great expanse of land below her, Wonder Woman took the long way around the world, stopping to redirect a tornado in Russia, put out a wildfire in Australia and save the koalas, and tidy up a massive landslide on Mount Fuji. But soon enough, she neared something that was perfect just the way it was.

The Amethyst's welcoming glow drew Wonder Woman to it, and when she saw Super Hero High, she knew in her heart that this was where she belonged.

However, not everyone felt the same way.

CHAPTER 2

Wonder Woman had flown all the way from Paradise Island, stopping only to lend a helping hand and for an occasional snack. She flew across serene seas and angry oceans, over mountains and valleys, through the Serengeti Plain, and along the Great Wall of China. But Wonder Woman had yet to encounter anything as epic, amazing, and scary as what she now saw directly below her.

High school.

Choreographed chaos commenced when a loud bell sounded. Instantly, throngs of students who had been milling about outside crashed through the doorway in a rush to get into the school. By the time Wonder Woman landed, only a few stragglers remained.

"Excuse me." Wonder Woman approached a girl dressed in layers of delicate faux-fur-lined cloth. She admired the ice-blue hair that swept the girl's shoulders. "Can you tell me where I might find Principal Amanda Waller?"

The girl looked Wonder Woman up and down and smirked at the newcomer's strange Amazonian warrior gear.

"Travel far?" the girl asked. Her eyes lingered on the small golden tiara with the ruby-red star nestled in Wonder Woman's messy hair, and she stared at the gleaming cuff bracelets on her wrists.

"Yes! I came all the way from Paradise Island," she answered. "I'm Wonder Woman!"

"Frost," the girl declared, clearly unimpressed.

Wonder Woman felt a sudden chill in the air. Frost tossed back her hair and pointed to the massive brick building. "Up the stairs, through the door, to the right, then to the left, and left, then right, then turn around and go back out again."

Wonder Woman blinked a few times. "Excuse me?"

"Kidding, just kidding," Frost said, dramatically tossing her hair once more and offering up a brilliant white smile. "Go inside and ask someone who cares."

"I'll do that!" Wonder Woman said brightly. "Thank you!"

"I'm Hawkgirl. May I help you?" the hall monitor asked. Her tidy brown hairdo matched her efficient personality. With a tilt of her head, the gray-feathered wings on her back folded close to her body. Wonder Woman admired her metal belt and harness with the head of a hawk carved in its center.

"Yes, please," Wonder Woman said. "Can you tell me

where I can find Principal Amanda Waller?"

"Down the hall, to the left," Hawkgirl informed her as she holstered her mace. "I'll take you there. Follow me." With that, Hawkgirl's wings opened once again to lift her off the ground and propel her toward the main building in the middle of campus.

"Thank you for caring," Wonder Woman called as she flew after her, smiling. Everyone was so helpful . . . and already hard to keep up with.

When she first entered the office, Wonder Woman slammed into a large bookcase. But she soon realized it wasn't a bookcase at all.

"Excuse you," Principal Waller said when she turned around. Dressed in a black power suit that complemented her dark skin and accentuated her strong shoulders, The Wall was an imposing figure. When she saw her newest student, the principal tried smiling warmly, once again giving off a look of digestive discomfort rather than welcome, before returning to her stern professional demeanor.

"Wonder Woman, let me be the first to welcome you to Super Hero High," Principal Waller said.

Wonder Woman didn't want to tell her that Frost had already been the first.

"Follow me," Principal Waller said, walking briskly. "We don't want to be late."

Principal Waller led Wonder Woman into the grand assembly hall. When Wonder Woman took a seat in the back, most of the kids in the auditorium turned around and stared at her. She was tickled to recognize several faces from the recruitment video. Not knowing what to do, Wonder Woman waved and then tossed her hair, as she had seen Frost do.

"Ahem!"

Principal Waller didn't need a microphone. As she stood onstage, her booming voice reached all the way to the back corners of the room and spilled outside to the student garden. When she spoke, students sat up and squirrels scattered.

"Today we are here to name our Hero of the Month," Principal Waller began. "As you know, this prestigious award goes to the teen super hero who has shown helpfulness, selflessness, and acted as a role model for all who attend Super Hero High School." Several students nodded confidently. Some wore elaborate super hero costumes, while others wore what looked almost like regular clothing. Wonder Woman admired a pale girl with flowing auburn hair and a vine of ivy woven through an elaborate side braid. The girl smiled shyly back, then motioned that Wonder Woman should be watching the stage.

"This month's Hero of the Month is . . . Bumblebee!"

A graceful teen with bronze skin and golden wings flew toward the stage as the audience broke out in cheers. Bumblebee's rich honey-colored boots matched the streaks in her curly brown hair, and her black leggings were accentuated with fancy patterned knee socks. Wonder Woman found herself applauding, too.

A video began to play. It showed Bumblebee shrinking to the size of an insect and projecting sonic blasts that mowed down a band of criminals intent on robbing Super Tunes music store, tutoring students in how to dodge bullets, and working in Principal Waller's office. The video ended with a teacher, Liberty Belle, saying, "Bumblebee's enthusiasm for learning is genuine. I only wish we had a whole hive of Bumblebees here!"

Wonder Woman saw the star logo at the close of the video and wrote on her to-do list *Become Hero of the Month*. Who wouldn't want that? She looked at the students sitting near her. The girl to her right was covered in silky fur with sleek spots. She stretched out slowly, as if bored. Wonder Woman smiled but was ignored. Thinking that perhaps she hadn't seen her, Wonder Woman poked the girl and said, "Hi, I'm Wonder Woman."

The girl glared at her and growled, "I'm Cheetah, and don't ever do that again."

"Okay!" Wonder Woman said, glancing over at the girl on her left. She recognized her from when she'd first landed.

Frost let a small smile slip out before she blew a freezing-cold blast of air at the green boy in front of her. As he sat frozen, Frost said, "Oops! Sorry. My bad," and laughed.

"Stop that!" someone ordered. An Asian girl leapt to her feet, chopping some of the icicles from the boy's clothes with her sword. Her jet-black hair was cut at a sharp angle, as if it had been sliced with a sword, too.

"Leave me alone, Katana," Frost said.

"You leave Beast Boy alone," Katana said, brandishing her gleaming silver sword. Wonder Woman could see her reflection in the blade.

Frost created a shield made of ice and held it up.

The two girls faced off in the aisle, glaring at each other as Beast Boy shape-shifted into the form of a penguin and said, "I'm all right, K-k-k-katana. I can handle the c-c-c-cold."

"Ahem!" Principal Waller called again.

"Great, now The Wall will be on our case," Frost whispered to Katana. "This is your fault."

"Students!" the principal bellowed. "You know the rules. No superpowers and no weapons during assembly. After-school detention for all of you!"

The teachers looked bored as they walked up and down the aisle, collecting wayward weapons in large metal bins. Amid the clanging sounds of swords and arrows and ammo being surrendered, Frost and Katana stewed and Beast Boy returned to his natural green form.

"Your belongings will be returned when you submit an essay on why it is a bad idea to bring your weapons or use your powers during assembly," Principal Waller said wearily before perking up.

"And now for some exciting news! The one hundredth Super hero Super Triathlon is taking place this year. I believe this is Super Hero High's year to shine. I won't go into details yet, but I *will* introduce the newest member of our student body. Wonder Woman, please join me."

Surprised and thrilled, Wonder Woman leapt into action, heading to the stage while waving and tossing her hair.

"Our newest student is a one-of-a-kind catch!" Principal Waller continued.

Catch? Wonder Woman thought. Was she supposed to catch something? She looked up in the air just as a student stuck her leg out.

"Who will catch you if you fall?" Cheetah asked with feigned innocence.

Wonder Woman stumbled, rolled into the fall, and jumped back up in one fluid motion. Students applauded. Cheetah scowled. Wonder Woman took a bow.

"Not the result you were expecting, is it?" someone sitting nearby said to Cheetah.

"Listen, Star Sapphire," Cheetah said. "If that girl thinks she's going to rule the school, she's wrong."

"You're right, of course," Star Sapphire said, toying with her shimmering sapphire ring.

Both looked at Wonder Woman, who had paused on her way to the stage. Cheetah was still scowling, but Wonder Woman only saw kindness on the other girl's face.

Soon enough, Wonder Woman was standing on the stage next to Principal Waller.

"We are all aware of your achievements, Wonder Woman," Waller was saying. "Most recently, rescuing those second graders. But what we are really looking forward to is what you can bring to Super Hero High to help inspire us. Would you care to say a few words?"

Wonder Woman looked out over the sea of super hero students. "It is I who came here to learn from all of you," she said earnestly. "There is so much good we can do in this world, and teaching each other is the first step."

Waller led the applause as Wonder Woman waved. Then the principal called Bumblebee back up to the stage. "Your first assignment as the current Hero of the Month is to show our new student around the school," she told her.

"Gladly!" Bumblebee said, offering Wonder Woman a warm, welcoming smile.

As the students jammed the hallways after the assembly, Bumblebee tried to weave in and out of the crowd, but her wings kept getting in her way. "You don't mind if I shrink, do you?" she asked.

Wonder Woman wasn't sure what that meant, but, not wanting to be rude, she said, "No. Please, go right ahead."

She watched as Bumblebee went from the size of a teenage girl to the size of—well, a bumblebee. As the Hero of the Month skillfully flew around the students who were ahead of her in the Flyers Only lane of the hallway, Wonder Woman found it difficult to keep up. Speed was not an issue, but flying while taking notes and pictures proved to be dangerous. "Sorry," she said when she veered out of the lane and knocked students down. "Oops! Sorry!"

"That's the library," Bumblebee said, pointing left.

"That's the dining hall," she said, pointing right. "And those are some of the fifty-six emergency exits," she said, pointing in all directions.

A swirl of gold and white skated past Wonder Woman. "Coming through!" the girl said brightly. Wonder Woman brushed some snowflakes off her dress and marveled as a sheet of ice appeared in front of the girl each time one of her skates touched the ground.

Wonder Woman caught up to Bumblebee, who was saying, "That's Golden Glider—" Wonder Woman wasn't listening, however. She had snapped into high alert.

A boy was heading straight toward her with his hand out. Was this an attack? In a lightning-fast offensive move, Wonder Woman rushed at him, grabbed his arm, whirled him around twice, and then tossed him down the hall, where he fell and skidded to an unattractive stop against the lockers.

Bumblebee circled, grew back to full size, and asked, "Um, why did you do that?"

Wonder Woman was still in her fighting pose, prepared for any other unknown enemies who might try to attack. "Just protecting myself, and you," she said, reaching for her Lasso of Truth before remembering that all weapons had been confiscated.

Bumblebee made herself small again and buzzed in Wonder Woman's ear, "He wasn't trying to hurt you. He was just going to shake your hand. Hal Jordan can be self-centered sometimes, but he's a Green Lantern and good guy."

This was confusing to Wonder Woman. He didn't look self-centered at all. If anything, he looked like he was only in the center of the floor. "Why would he try to shake my hand?" she asked. "There's nothing wrong with it."

"It's what polite people do when they greet each other," Bumblebee explained.

Wonder Woman felt silly. In a flash she was leaning over Green Lantern while he tried to sit up. There was going to be a big bump from where his head had hit the locker. *Boys are so strange,* Wonder Woman thought as she stared at him. She had never seen one up close like this before. His short, thick brown hair and dimpled jaw were accentuated with an attention-grabbing mega-zit. *Do all boys have pimples?*

Hal saw Wonder Woman staring, and he started to cover the zit when she suddenly grabbed his right hand.

"So sorry for that," she said. "I'm Wonder Woman. Nice to meet you."

Super Hero High's newest student shook Green Lantern's hand vigorously.

"Ow, ow, ow!" he cried, taking his hand back and examining it for bruises.

Wonder Woman looked at him expectantly. What was he trying to tell her? Did boys speak in code? *Ow, ow, ow?*

Embarrassed, Green Lantern said, "Ow . . . um, 'ow are you?"

Wonder Woman smiled. She liked the way he talked. "I'm just fine!" she said. "'Ow are you?"

CHAPTER 3

In her first class of her first day at Super Hero High, Wonder Woman wanted to remember everything so she could write to her mother about it. During Flyers' Ed, she watched in awe as Beast Boy morphed into a large double-crested cormorant, a fishing bird, before her eyes. She was heartened to see he had completely thawed out, even if he did still waddle a bit.

As a bird, Beast Boy's takeoff was superb—but suddenly, in midair, something went wrong. He turned back into a green-skinned teen and plunged toward the ground. As Wonder Woman positioned herself for the catch, Beast Boy shape-shifted into a flying squirrel, did three in-flight somersaults, and landed safely at her feet.

"Gotcha!" he said, laughing when he turned back into a boy.

"Beast Boy!" the teacher, Red Tornado, barked, his face looking even redder than usual. For a synthetic man with artificial intelligence, he had no problem letting people know how he felt. "What did I tell you about false flight failures?"

"False flight failures are not funny," Beast Boy said, hanging his head and looking remorseful. He winked at Wonder Woman and whispered, "But they are!"

Wonder Woman was impressed and confused by what she had just seen. She took a picture of Beast Boy before grabbing his right hand and energetically shaking it. "Hello! I'm Wonder Woman," she said. "That was amazing!"

Wonder Woman noticed the class staring at her. Then she felt embarrassed. How could she have been so rude? Starting with Red Tornado, Wonder Woman quickly went around the room, shaking everyone's hand, telling them her name, and waving and tossing her hair. By the time she got to the last student, the unassuming girl said in barely a whisper, "I'm Miss Martian." Before Wonder Woman could greet her, the girl turned invisible, leaving Wonder Woman with her hand extended to no one.

"That was fun," she said to Bumblebee, who looked like she was trying to suppress a giggle. Wonder Woman couldn't wait until she got her class assignments. As her school tour continued, Wonder Woman became particularly smitten with SaveBall, a game the Supers were playing in phys ed.

"Throw to the team captain!" the teacher yelled.

"What's a team captain?" she asked Bumblebee. Half the field cheered when Cyborg tossed a robotic dummy into a net.

"It means you're in charge," she answered.

Wonder Woman made a note of that. *Be team captain. Be in charge.*

As they made their way down the hall, Wonder Woman straightened the portraits of the famous super hero alumni lining the walls, picked up trash, and fixed a warped metal banister.

"Wow," Bumblebee said. "That's been bent out of shape ever since Firestorm accidentally melted it. Everyone always said it looked bad, but you're the first person to do something about it."

"Wonder Woman, over here!" someone called.

"That's Barbara Gordon," Bumblebee explained, motioning to the girl standing next to a bank of lockers, some low, others ten feet up near the ceiling. "She's a tech whiz from Gotham City High who helps out around the school. Her dad's one of the teachers here."

"Wonder Woman, that one's yours," Barbara said, taking a slip of paper from her clipboard. "Flyers always get the top lockers."

Wonder Woman looked at the series of numbers written neatly on the paper. She wished her handwriting was half as nice, but she had a habit of pressing too hard on the paper and was always snapping the tips of her pencils off.

"Is this to break into a safe?" Wonder Woman whispered. Back home, she loved reading about bank robbers and other unsavory criminals in her *Tragic & Totally True*

Colossal Crimes comics. Hippolyta wasn't thrilled about her daughter's choice of reading materials, preferring that she read textbooks, flight manuals, and how-to tomes on warrior skills. Wonder Woman had to hide her stash of comics under her spare weapons, and often read them at night under her covers with a flashlight.

Barbara laughed good-naturedly. "It's not quite the combination to a safe," she said, pushing her dark ginger bangs out of her eyes. "It's your locker combination. My dad, Commissioner Gordon, says one can never be too careful, so keep your combo a secret. Here's how it works. Watch."

Barbara pulled a grappling hook from her tool belt and climbed to the top locker. When the door popped open, Wonder Woman's eyes became misty. Her very own locker!

"What could be better than this?" she said as she took a photo of it.

"I'll show you," Bumblebee said brightly. "Follow me!"

As they flew past the nurse's station there was a long line of students holding their right hands and grimacing. Wonder Woman smiled and waved to them, calling out each student's name. Some flinched when they saw her. But most seemed pleased that Wonder Woman had remembered them.

"Wait!" Wonder Woman said as they passed The Wall's office. "I want to drop off my essay."

Bumblebee blinked in surprise. "You finished your essay already?" she asked.

"Yes," Wonder Woman said, waving it in the air. "To get our weapons back, right?"

"But when did you write it?"

"While we were walking from class to class," said Wonder Woman. With her Lasso of Truth back in her hands, Wonder Woman followed Bumblebee down a maze of stairs, through secret passageways, and up to a brick wall. She tapped it three times, and to Wonder Woman's delight, the wall spun inward, revealing an opening.

Three, Wonder Woman wrote in her notes.

"Welcome to the girls' dorm," Bumblebee announced.

Wonder Woman's eyes grew wide. She could hardly contain her excitement. She had never lived in a dorm. She had never lived *anywhere* other than Paradise Island. Wonder Woman couldn't wait to meet her roommates.

Just as she was about to go into Room #27, Wonder Woman froze. Someone was shouting, "When is Wonder Woman going to get here? I can't wait to shoot her!"

CHAPTER 4

Knowing that the element of surprise was crucial to thwarting any attack, Wonder Woman kicked down the door and leapt inside. Shocked by the scene that lay before her, she gasped. The room looked like it had been ransacked. Wonder Woman had never seen such chaos!

Piles of clothes and junk were strewn everywhere. A television was blasting, and so was a music video on the computer. A damp beach towel hung from the curtain rod. Camera equipment was scattered about. Empty potato chip bags were piled on papers that were piled on books that were piled on one of the beds. Wonder Woman assumed, at least, that there was a bed under it all.

"She's here!" someone yelled.

Wonder Woman whipped around, and in a nanosecond, the girl was wrapped in the Lasso of Truth. She dropped her video camera and gushed, "I was waiting for you."

Bumblebee, now tiny, flew into the room and landed on

Wonder Woman's shoulder. Before she could say anything, Wonder Woman demanded, "Who are you and what do you want?"

Entangled in the Lasso of Truth, the girl had no choice but to be honest. "My name is Harley Quinn, and I want to shoot a video of you for my station, HQTV," she said, then added, "and I am totally extremely super excited to be your roommate!"

That was when Wonder Woman recognized her. Of course! She was the blond girl in almost every scene in the Super Hero High School recruitment video. The circus-colored pigtails, the giant smile, the mischievous twinkle in her eyes. Wonder Woman released Harley and apologized.

Much to Wonder Woman's surprise, Harley was far from being angry. She was thrilled, and let out a long, loud laugh.

"I was just talking to the camera, saying I wanted to shoot you, and then BAM, you rock the room! And . . . and then you throw your famous lasso at me! ME! The best part is I caught it all here!" Harley raised her camera into the air like it was a trophy. "Exclusive footage, that's what I have. An HQTV exclusive! So great to meet you, Wonder Woman!"

When Harley extended her hand, Wonder Woman shook it with such enthusiasm that Harley's head bounced back and forth like a bobblehead doll. But Harley Quinn didn't look fazed.

"Excuse me?" The buzz got louder until Bumblebee was back to her full size.

Wonder Woman had forgotten that Bumblebee was in the room. She had been so small and so quiet.

"I've got to tackle my homework," Bumblebee said. She motioned to Wonder Woman and told Harley, "She already wrote her paper on why weapons shouldn't be allowed in assemblies and handed it in!"

Harley nodded knowingly. "Not surprised, not surprised," she said. "Keep doing things like that, and you're sure to be every teacher's pet!"

Wonder Woman tilted her head to one side. "But I'm not an animal—I'm a girl," she said earnestly.

Harley let out another signature laugh. "Funny!" she said. "You're a regular comedian! I love that."

"Oh! No, I'm not a comedian, I'm a super hero," Wonder Woman said.

"It's a joke," Harley said. "Ha, ha. You know, a joke?" When Wonder Woman stared blankly at her, she said, "Aw, don't be so serious. Come on, get a sense of humor!"

"Okay," Wonder Woman said. She wrote on her to-do list *Get a sense of humor.*

As Harley prattled on about how they would be the best roommates in the history of Super Hero High, Wonder Woman surveyed the room. With super-fast skills, she began to tidy up, tossing out trash, straightening books, and rearranging the furniture. When she lifted a pile of Harley's belongings off her bed, she realized it wasn't a bed at all—it was a trampoline!

"So then—this Mandy Bowin was a real case," Harley was saying as she edited her video with the finesse of a master playing the piano. "She was this really quiet kid. Nice, but couldn't take a joke, if you know what I mean. One time I hid her violin and she went ballistic! And get this, it was a regular violin, not even a weapon. Mandy and her music. It was like twenty-four/seven. She didn't even have a super hero name, just plain Mandy. *Everyone* here has a super hero name."

Harley did a double backflip, bounced on the bed, and then sat back down, continuing to edit her video.

"So then," Harley said, "one day, BAM! Mandy's gone and you're here. Done editing! Yes, I'm that fast." Harley stood and looked around the room. "Wow, wow, wow! And did I say, wow?"

It was spotless. And practically empty.

Wonder Woman smiled modestly. "I cleaned our room," she said.

"Where's all my stuff?" Harley asked, looking under the beds.

"In the trash," Wonder Woman answered.

"I don't know what to say . . . ," Harley began.

"It was my pleasure," Wonder Woman said. "Um, could you tell me where the bathroom is?"

Harley pointed. "Down the hall, to the left. And hurry back—dinner is soon."

"Will do!" Wonder Woman said.

When she returned, Wonder Woman found her roommate sitting crossed-legged on her trampoline bed, designing some graphics on her computer. Their room, which Wonder Woman had just cleaned, was already a mess again.

"Did you use a time-warp machine to get the room to go back to the way it was?" she asked.

"Nope," Harley said cheerfully. "I just put a few of my personal belongings back where they were." Wonder Woman looked at the bulletin board, which was newly cluttered with photos and pages from magazines. One of the posters read:

The Three POWS!

Super-POWer

Brain-POWer

Will-POWer

Wonder Woman wondered if her new roommate had super powers. She was certainly a force of nature.

CHAPTER 5

The hustle and bustle in the dining hall had Wonder Woman feeling momentarily discombobulated. The constant clanging of silverware, the students rushing around gripping brown plastic trays, and the nonstop chatter that echoed off the high ceilings were unlike anything Wonder Woman had ever experienced. At one end of the room was a long row of confusing foods with steam rising from their metal bins, dished out by women wearing white smocks and yellow plastic gloves. You only had to point to something and it was unceremoniously plopped onto your plate.

Wonder Woman loved it.

As she held her tray of mystery food, Wonder Woman was so busy looking around at the heavy wooden tables and the fancy modern light fixtures overhead that– BUMP!

"Hey! Watch where you're going," a girl said, wiping gray gravy from her violet blouse. Some of the gravy had managed to get on her matching skirt, too.

"I am so sorry," Wonder Woman said. "Truly and honestly sorry. I'm Wonder Woman." She took the girl's hand to shake it, but the girl pulled it back.

"I know who you are," the girl said. "I'm Star Sapphire. My family owns Ferris Aircraft. They could probably buy ten Paradise Islands if they wanted to."

"Oh, but there's only one, and it's not for sale," Wonder Woman informed her helpfully.

Star Sapphire shook her head. "Darling, get a clue."

Even though Star Sapphire's words were harsh, Wonder Woman felt a wave of warmth wash over her. She wrote on her to-do list *Get a clue.*

"Why do you have gravy all over yourself?" Golden Glider asked Star Sapphire as she skated up and handed her a napkin. The sparkly headband holding back her mass of blond hair said LIVE. Wonder Woman admired the smooth sheets of ice Golden Glider's skates created.

Star Sapphire smirked. "Gravy is not my accessory of choice, but apparently Wonder Woman thought otherwise. Thank you, Wonder Woman."

"You're welcome!" Wonder Woman said, relieved that Star Sapphire wasn't mad at her.

"Let's get out of here," Star Sapphire said to Golden Glider.

"Anything you say," Golden Glider replied, and the girls turned their backs on Wonder Woman.

"Goodbye," Wonder Woman said to the empty space

where Golden Glider and Star Sapphire had once stood.

All the tables were full. As Super Hero High's newest member wandered around, most of the students smiled at her or said hello, and some of the boys just stared. To alleviate the awkwardness, Wonder Woman told Green Lantern, "You have food in your teeth," and to Cyborg she said cheerfully, "Be careful with that drink, or the metal in your head could rust."

But when the Riddler asked, "Want to hear a riddle?" Wonder Woman answered, "Yes, I do!" and kept walking, looking for a place to sit. She did want to hear one. Just not right then.

Just when Wonder Woman began to think she'd have to eat standing up, Bumblebee waved to her. "Sit with us!" she called, motioning to an empty seat.

Wonder Woman rushed over and happily took the chair next to Katana, whom she recognized from the assembly.

"Is spilling gravy on someone a really bad thing?" Wonder Woman asked.

"Depends on who," Bumblebee said, drizzling honey into her tea.

"Star Sapphire," Wonder Woman reported.

Katana burst out laughing. Wonder Woman did, too, though she wasn't sure what was so funny.

"She's quite the fashionista and wears the latest trends, the kind most kids aspire to," Katana said, glancing at Star

Sapphire, who was still trying to get the gravy off her clothes. "I prefer cutting-edge styles, myself. Less is more."

Wonder Woman took note. While Star Sapphire wore sparkles and bright colors, Katana was dressed in sleek, muted shades of gray with a dash of red.

Bumblebee continued to pour extra honey into her drink. "I like clothes that can stretch and shrink when I do," she said, adding with a laugh, "I learned that the hard way!"

"I like dark colors," Katana said, picking up her fork and knife. Before Wonder Woman could blink, Katana had sliced up all the food on her plate. "So I can be stealthy."

Hawkgirl put her tray down on the table. "May we join you?" she asked. Someone with red hair stood behind her.

"Yes! Please do!" Wonder Woman said, delighted to be in the company of more super heroes. "We were just discussing clothes!"

"I don't give them much thought," Hawkgirl said, then she drained a glass of milk. "They need to be practical so I can fly, and sturdy so I can fight."

"What about you?" Wonder Woman asked the red-haired girl, who wore an emerald-green dress.

The girl blushed the color of her hair. "I'm Poison Ivy," she said, not meeting Wonder Woman's steady gaze. "I love plants, and green lets me blend in with them."

"You look good in green," Wonder Woman said brightly. "Doesn't she?"

Everyone nodded, and by the time lunch was over, the girls were talking and laughing as if they'd been friends forever.

"Wonder Woman, what are you doing?" Katana asked when dinner was done.

"Cleaning up," Wonder Woman answered. With lightning-fast speed, she had already wiped down half the tables in the huge room.

Katana shook her head. "That's not necessary. There's staff to do that."

Wonder Woman looked around and saw a small group of people in blue uniforms mopping the floor and scrubbing the tables. She left the dining hall with her new friends, but after they parted, Wonder Woman went back.

"Hey, Wonder Woman there's no need to help us," one of the men in blue said. His head was bald, his skin was purple, and his smile was genuine. Sewn above the pocket of his janitor uniform in fancy script was the name Parasite.

"I don't mind," Wonder Woman said, grabbing a mop.

"Really," Parasite said, wrestling the mop back. "You go back to your studies. That's what you're here for. But we appreciate your offer."

Wonder Woman nodded. But before she left, she called back to the crew, "If you ever need any help, I'm here!"

She had just made more friends.

Wonder Woman had only brought a few things from home, but none of them were where she had left them when she got back to her room.

Harley, who should have been finishing up her Heroes Throughout History assignment, was monitoring the viewer counts on her latest HQTV post—featuring herself. "Look!" she said, jumping up and down on her bed. "We're famous! FAMOUS! The video of you throwing your lasso around me has gone viral!"

Wonder Woman wasn't sure whether to be pleased or embarrassed. When she'd left for Super Hero High, Hippolyta had told her daughter to take fame in stride. "Don't ever let your ego get in the way of your strength," she'd said.

"Harley, do you know where my pillow is?" Wonder Woman asked, looking around.

"In the garbage," Harley said, returning to her TV channel.

"Oh, okay," Wonder Woman said. "Did you put it there?"

"Nope," Harley answered. She was now doing backflips. "It was there when I got back from dinner. I thought you'd put it there."

Sure enough, everything was in the trash, including her pillow. As Wonder Woman pulled out her belongings, she came across an envelope addressed to her. Seeing the familiar handwriting, Wonder Woman felt a pang of homesickness. So much had happened in one day, she'd almost forgotten that this would be her first night away from home. Unless, of course, she counted Paradise Island Warrior Summer Camp.

Her first night there, she had cried and called her mother, begging for her to come get her.

"If you feel the same way in two days, I will," her mother promised.

Wonder Woman cried one more time that week—on the day camp was over and she had to leave.

As she slipped between her sheets, Wonder Woman realized how exhausted she was. "Harley," she asked, "what happened to your last roommate?"

Harley had a sleep mask over her eyes. When she didn't answer, Wonder Woman assumed she was asleep.

Wonder Woman stretched out on her bed. The mattress was hard. She was glad she had brought her pillow—it reminded her of home. Just as Wonder Woman closed her eyes, she heard Harley say, "There are rumors that Mandy was expelled, and wasn't happy about it. She threatened to come back and cause trouble."

Wonder Woman's eyes opened.

"Cheetah says she was kicked out to make room for you," Harley continued. "She says The Wall wanted you here, so goodbye, Mandy; hello, Wonder Woman. But that's not true. Everyone knows that if you've got great potential, Waller will move mountains to make room for you here." Wonder Woman lay still, hoping Harley would say more. "My guess? Mandy didn't have what it takes. Instead of working on her weapons, all she wanted to do was play her violin. How painful was that for me to listen to day and night, night and day?"

"Well, music is . . ." But before Wonder Woman could finish her sentence, Harley was snoring. And sleep-talking. And snoring.

Wonder Woman sat up. She suddenly wasn't tired anymore. As much as she had wanted to attend Super Hero High, she didn't want to do it at the expense of another student. What if Cheetah was right? Or what if Harley was right, and Mandy was expelled for not having what it takes to be a super hero? That could happen to *her*! Wonder Woman wished her mother were there. She always knew the right thing to say.

Then Wonder Woman remembered the envelope. Inside was a note. *My dearest daughter,* it began, *though it saddens me that you have left Paradise Island, I am happy that you are finding your place in the world. Be strong. I love you. Never forget that.*

Tucked inside the envelope was a photo of her mother and Wonder Woman when she was little. They were wearing their matching white Greek goddess tunics. Hippolyta was holding up a boulder, and a young Wonder Woman was standing on it, holding up a smaller boulder.

Wonder Woman's eyes misted up as she stared at the photo. Just because she was a super hero, it didn't mean she couldn't miss her mom.

CHAPTER 6

". . . and so I thank all of you for electing me as your president," Wonder Woman said as she stood on the steps of the White House.

The crowd, dressed in Wonder Woman shirts, cheered and waved **WW FOR PRESIDENT** banners. "My first priority as your president will be world peace," she promised. "And now I'll take questions from the reporters."

"Are you a morning person or a night person?" Harley Quinn asked.

"Excuse me?"

"Morning or night person?" Harley pressed.

Wonder Woman blinked and sat up. She had sleep in her eyes—that crusty stuff that was almost as annoying as the video camera in her face. "Was I dreaming?" Wonder Woman asked, and she rubbed her eyes vigorously.

"Not sure," Harley said as she adjusted the video lens. "You're a solid sleeper, although there was a lot of waving going on. But my viewers want to know more about you, so . . ."

"Morning person," Wonder Woman said, now fully awake. She bounded up, and in one sweeping gesture, made her bed. Then, while she was at it, she made her roommate's trampoline bed, too, as Harley filmed her.

Wonder Woman brushed her hair, adjusted her tiara, and then looked around for her bracelets. She was dismayed to find them on her roommate's wrists, and to see that Harley was now tangled up in her lasso.

"Harley, what are you doing?" Wonder Woman asked.

"I wanted to see what it would be like to be you," Harley said.

As Wonder Woman unraveled her roommate, Harley became more animated. "Okay! Well, that was fun. Wowza! Now let me post the video of you waking up. I know my viewers are going to want to see that!"

Wonder Woman bit her lip. "It might be boring," she said. "Perhaps you could put someone else on HQTV."

"That's just what I was thinking!" Harley said, leaping up and doing a somersault to prove her point. "I've added a familiar face. Watch!"

As the theme music began to rise, the usual HQTV logo had a new twist: Harley's laughing face appeared on-screen in the middle of the *Q*.

"Oh! And don't worry, it's not just you on HQTV," Harley assured her. "I shoot everyone!"

To prove her point, Harley showed Wonder Woman a clip of Frost freezing Miss Martian's hot soup, and another one of the Riddler refusing to let anyone into the library until they could answer his riddle.

Wonder Woman wasn't sure that made her feel any better, but she didn't want to upset Harley. Plus it was her first full day as a student at Super Hero High. She was determined to make a good impression.

"Is it true that you're a lock for the Super Triathlon team?" Harley asked as she uploaded the video.

Wonder Woman was reading her emails. There were several from her mother.

"A lock?" she asked. She shook her head. "I don't think I'm a lock; I'm more of a girl—you know, a super hero girl."

"No, no," Harley sighed. "Man, are you literal. I mean a shoo-in to be on the team."

Wonder Woman pondered the question. To her, it seemed that her roommate spoke in gibberish, asking if she was a lock or a shoe. "I'm just me," she said, finally. "And it would be an honor to be on the team."

"Well, you know our school hasn't won in fifty years, right? We've come in second and third, but Waller wants the gold. Everyone's talking about who will be on the team. The stakes are pretty high, especially because this is the Super Triath's one hundredth year. That means whichever school wins becomes the place to be."

Wonder Woman nodded. She was listening, but not

truly paying attention. She was focused on an email from an anonymous sender. It read *You are not wanted at Super Hero High. Go home.*

". . . and so," Harley was saying as she bounced on her just-made bed, "every school in the galaxy wanted you, and everyone at Super Hero High wanted you to come here!"

Wonder Woman turned off her computer. *Not everyone,* she thought.

If Wonder Woman's mother had taught her anything, it was to never feel sorry for herself. Though she was a princess, Wonder Woman didn't act like one—or live like one. She was used to eating a simple breakfast of roasted berries and nutritious plants. That morning in the cafeteria, a wall of color stopped Wonder Woman in her tracks.

"If you look at it long enough, it'll talk to you," Cheetah murmured as she passed Wonder Woman.

Wonder Woman stared hard at the colors. What would they say to her, she wondered? Maybe she should say something first.

"You're so pretty," Wonder Woman gushed.

Poison Ivy looked around, unsure. "Me?"

"No, that," Wonder Woman said pointing to the bright colors in fanciful shapes that were housed in a huge wall of glass containers.

"What? Oh, the cereal?" Poison Ivy asked, looking momentarily crestfallen. She handed Wonder Woman a bowl. "Fill it up," she said. "Well, if you want to. I mean, you don't have to. Oh, never mind. Sorry. Just forget I'm here."

"Why would I want to do that?" Wonder Woman asked. "I like your idea of filling up the bowl!"

Poison Ivy smiled.

Not sure which cereal to try, Wonder Woman decided to eat them all. For research, of course. She took her place at the table, balancing eight full bowls. The talk was lively, and ranged from the new custom weapon Lady Shiva had ordered online to the plight of the indigenous life-forms on the planet Rann to whether Barry "The Flash" Allen was really as fast as he claimed to be.

"HELLO!" All heads turned to Harley. "Who wants to see my latest HQTV video? All of you? Yes! Thought so. It's already racked up hundreds of hits. Watch!"

Everyone squeezed in to see a sleepy and confused Wonder Woman wake up to a camera in her face and mumble. The short video was titled *Sleeping Beauty.* As the girls laughed, Wonder Woman smiled awkwardly. Did they think she was funny? Did they think she was weird? Wonder Woman wasn't sure what they thought, so she kept smiling, even though it was starting to hurt.

★

Wonder Woman had thoroughly enjoyed the colorful sugary cereals. She ate them all, not wanting one bit of crunchy goodness to go to waste. By the time breakfast was over, she was chock-full of energy and raring to go!

Wonder Woman's first class was Flyers' Ed. The Flight Track was housed under a huge clear dome that opened with the press of a button. That way, when the Supers wanted to fly even higher, or when they were doing side-by-side formation stunt flights—always a favorite on Parents' Night—they had that option. On the sides of the dome, missiles, assorted asteroids, and various projectiles stood by for defensive flying practice. Up above, storm, hail, and lightning machines were at the ready.

"Wonder Woman! Welcome, welcome," cried the famed flyer and flying teacher, Red Tornado. "Such an honor to have the daughter of Amazon Queen Hippolyta in my class. You know I met your mother once at Super Summit CLXXVII, and though I doubt she'd remember me, I sure remember her." Red Tornado stopped to catch his breath and seemed to float into a momentary daydream as he looked off into the sky. He coughed and brought himself back down to earth. "Do tell your dear mother that Red says hi!"

Wonder Woman made a note on her to-do list.

"Teacher's pet," someone whispered so loudly that the whole class heard.

Wonder Woman looked around eagerly for an animal or alien pet, but didn't see one. She had always wanted a

Wallaroo, but her mother said they were too hard to take care of.

"I will be training the flyers for our Super Triathlon team. Though no one is guaranteed a spot, I can only guess who might make the cut," Red Tornado said. "It might even be someone in this class!" He winked at Wonder Woman.

Unsure what to do, she winked back. Some of the other students gave each other sideways glances. Frost and Cheetah winked at the new girl, and Wonder Woman winked at them, too, and then winked at the rest of the class, who all winked back at her.

"Eyes on me!" Red Tornado ordered as he spun into the air, creating an actual red tornado. "Nonflyers to the side!"

"Why are they splitting us up?" Wonder Woman asked Hawkgirl, who had just flexed her impressive wings.

"Nonflyers are here to observe and gain insight into flight patterns, aerodynamics, and navigation," Hawkgirl whispered. "It could help them in battle."

As he'd heard, Red Tornado said, "Always be on the offense. Know your enemy and anticipate what they will do! Okay, first up! Who will volunteer?"

Beast Boy began to step forward, but he wasn't as fast as Star Sapphire. "Harness!" she commanded. The violet ring on her finger began to glow.

Instantly, Miss Martian, who was the harness helper for the day, hooked her up to the special safety belt that was controlled remotely by Red Tornado. As Star Sapphire gracefully rose into the sky, she struck midair glamour poses. Even from a distance, Wonder Woman could see the glow of her ring, which sent a wash of purple pastel onto the students below.

"She's so amazing," Wonder Woman said, not able to take her eyes off Star Sapphire and the haze of purple around her. "I wish I were more like her."

"I think I love her," Beast Boy said, staring up. "And I'm fairly certain that Star Sapphire loves me, too."

Katana, who was standing in the shadow of an old stealth bomber, shook her head and snorted. "You're both delusional. Star Sapphire is so full of herself. Rumor has it that she's trying to convince her parents that she belongs on the cover of *Super Hero Super Model* magazine and has been begging them to buy the company."

"She'd look good on the cover," Wonder Woman mused. Beast Boy nodded in agreement.

Next up was Hawkgirl. Wonder Woman, still full of sugary cereal goodness, bounced in place. *This is so much fun!* she thought. Hawkgirl did a precision flight and landing, proving herself to be an advanced flyer.

As the class continued, there were some spectacular accidents. If not for the safety harness, a full 50 percent or more of the flyers would have ended up in the emergency room. While most students applauded the efforts of their peers, nonflyers Frost, Cheetah, and Golden Glider were more content critiquing their classmates.

When it was Bumblebee's turn, she made a flawless lap around the flying course. Wonder Woman jumped up and down and cheered, while Frost and Cheetah stayed noticeably silent.

"Our next flyer," Red Tornado announced, "can probably teach you a thing or two. Take notes, class. Take notes!"

Wonder Woman took out her notepad and looked around, eager to watch and learn. When no one stepped forward, she felt the awkward silence in the room.

Red Tornado cleared his throat and nodded at her. Wonder Woman cleared her throat and nodded back. He tilted his head toward the flying course, and Wonder Woman did the same.

"You're up, Wonder Woman," he finally said, straightening his cape.

"Me?" she asked, surprised. "Okay, here I go," she said.

Just as she was about to take off, a loud alarm sounded. Wonder Woman stepped back. What had she done? The alarm wouldn't stop.

"Save the Day alarm!" Bumblebee shouted. She flew down the hallways, alerting everyone.

"Save the Day!" a voice intoned over the PA system.

Before Wonder Woman could ask what they were supposed to do, everyone had disappeared, leaving her alone on the Flight Track.

Wonder Woman went outside to see what all the commotion was about. She only saw a flood of Supers heading toward her. They were all talking animatedly. From what she could pick up, Golden Glider was about to skate to victory, when The Flash swept in and saved the day.

"It's a test," Bumblebee explained as she linked her arm with Wonder Woman's on their way back to class. "Save the Day is a drill to see if we know what to do in an emergency. Today the teachers hurled poisonous projectiles toward a vacant bank. It was just for practice, but you never know when a real alarm is going to sound."

Wonder Woman hoped that sometime she'd be able to save the day. In the meantime, she still needed to show Red Tornado what she could do.

As Wonder Woman approached the takeoff pad, Cheetah gave her a slow smile. "No pressure," she said, "but your mom is famous for flying, and if you don't fly flawlessly, you'll let her down. Oh, and look—there's Harley!"

Harley waved to Wonder Woman and held up her camera.

Wonder Woman thought of her mother. She had promised her that she would make her proud, but she'd never flown this course before. The sugar from breakfast suddenly wore off, and instead of a sugary high, Wonder Woman was faced with a crashing uncertainty.

"Take your mark, Wonder Woman," Red Tornado called. "Ready to be spectacular?" He didn't wait for her answer. "Okay, let's show them how it's done! Three, two, one . . . take off!"

51

CHAPTER 7

All eyes were on Super Hero High's newest student, the one they had heard so much about. The one who was supposed to bring the school to a Super Triathlon victory. The one . . . the only . . .

Wonder Woman stepped onto the takeoff pad. She fastened her safety harness, even though she was certain she wouldn't need it. Other than the low buzzing sound from Bumblebee, who had made herself tiny, there was silence on the Ferris Flight Track.

Red Tornado could hardly contain himself. He took a deep breath, then shouted, "TAKE OFF!"

In a heartbeat, Wonder Woman was flying. As she soared high into the air, her classmates look stunned by what they were seeing. Some gasped. Others gawked. It was spectacular.

Spectacularly bad.

As she ping-ponged back and forth on the Flight Track, hitting the clear poly-strength ultra-rubber sidewalls fortified with titanium trellis beams, Wonder Woman struggled to gain control. She had miscalculated her takeoff, rising far too quickly. But as she tried to adjust midair, a glint from below momentarily blinded her. Distracted, all Wonder Woman could think of was what Cheetah had said about her mother: *"If you don't fly flawlessly, you'll let her down."*

From high in the air, it looked like everyone was twirling around on the ground. *Or maybe I'm the one who's spinning,* Wonder Woman thought. The only person she could make out clearly was Red Tornado, and he looked like he had just eaten a lemon, or maybe two. The more she thought about her teacher and what he must think of her, the worse Wonder Woman's flying became. Finally, he blew his whistle and reined Wonder Woman in with the remote-controlled safety harness. It was, as the whispers echoed, "a disaster."

None of her fellow flyers would meet her eyes, and when she glanced at the nonflyers, only Cheetah and Frost looked back. Cheetah winked at Wonder Woman while Frost turned to her compact mirror and applied her blue lipstick.

Miss Martian unhooked the safety harness in silence, turning invisible to avoid having to say anything to Wonder Woman about her ill-fated flight.

"It's happened to all of us," Hawkgirl said, trying to comfort her friend.

"I mess up all the time," Bumblebee assured her, even though Wonder Woman knew she was just trying to console her. Harley had told her that even though Bumblebee's parents were not super heroes, the super hero suit she'd built—coupled with her unique DNA—made her an excellent flyer. "And with everyone watching," Bumblebee continued generously, "well, it's no surprise that you'd get nervous."

The weird thing, though, was that Wonder Woman hadn't been nervous. Sure, she'd ascended too quickly, but she had done that in the past when miscalculating headwinds, migrating birds, and low-flying spacecraft. But this time, Wonder Woman had been unable to self-correct, and she'd let self-doubt take over. How was she ever going to save the world if she couldn't even fly straight?

Just then, Wonder Woman noticed Harley waving to her and holding her camera in the air. "Got it!" Harley shouted. "The W-Threes are gonna love this!"

"The who?" Wonder Woman asked. Her shoulders slumped.

"The WWWs, the W-Threes—the Wonder Woman Watchers. I've got millions of them! Or maybe hundreds, but that'll change. They love my exclusive videos of you. My goal is to bring my numbers up, and with your help, HQTV will be a media darling! You are my not-so-secret weapon!"

Wonder Woman didn't want to be a not-so-secret weapon, but her mother had told her that as a super hero, she was a role model, and being in the news was just part of the job.

"It's information and entertainment," Harley explained, executing a double backflip while still holding her camera. "I'm doing a service for the community with my videos. If you can't attend Super Hero High, at least you can watch what happens there!"

Wonder Woman noticed a serious-looking girl standing on the sidelines, taking notes. Her black hair ran past her shoulders, and she was wearing a crisp white T-shirt and clean, cuffed jeans.

"I like your necklace," Wonder Woman said. When the girl smiled, she didn't look serious at all. She looked warm and friendly.

"Thank you," she said, "but do you want to know a secret?"

Wonder Woman nodded.

"It's not a necklace . . . it's my press pass."

While Wonder Woman pondered that, the girl extended her hand. "I'm Lois Lane. I'm a reporter from Metropolis High, and I cover the super hero beat. You can find my articles on my *Super News* website. Whoa!" Lois suddenly exclaimed. "That's quite a handshake you have there. Maybe you should go easy on us mortals!"

As she blinked back the pain, Lois asked, "Would you be up for an interview sometime? Metropolis citizens want to know all about the new super hero who's going to school in the middle of their city. What do you say? I'll treat you to the best fruit smoothie and sweet potato fries you've ever had."

Wonder Woman really didn't want any more media attention, but Lois Lane seemed nice and, well, she'd never tried sweet potato fries. Would they taste sugary, like her cereal? "Sure," Wonder Woman said, then paused. "Are you going to write about me messing up in flight class?"

Lois Lane shook her head. "I'm sure we can come up with more interesting stuff than that."

"Thank you," Wonder Woman said gratefully. She wished she could tell Harley to stop airing her videos. But Wonder Woman wasn't one to boss someone around . . . unless, of course, it was required for saving the world.

Trying to put her disastrous flight behind her, Wonder Woman was looking forward to her Heroes Throughout History class. *"Knowing the past can help us prepare for the future,"* her mother always said.

"Over here!" Katana called out.

Wonder Woman made her way toward her friends, careful not to trip over the weapons that were left in the aisles. As she sat down, she was surprised to find a note on her desk. She looked around, not sure what to do with it. She hoped it wasn't a message like the one she'd received that morning, telling her she wasn't welcome at Super Hero High.

"Open it," Poison Ivy mouthed.

Wonder Woman cautiously unfolded the piece of paper. She smiled when she saw what was inside—a drawing of the five of them: Poison Ivy, Hawkgirl, Katana, Bumblebee, and Wonder Woman, with the caption **FABULOUS 5!!!** And when she looked around, her friends were smiling back at her.

"Fabulous Five?" Wonder Woman asked.

"It could be our team name. Um, maybe," Poison Ivy said, her cheeks turning a shade of pink that matched the flower pin she was wearing.

"Eyes up here, class!" Liberty Belle said, ringing a miniature Liberty Bell that sat on her desk.

Wonder Woman tucked the piece of paper into her pocket. She wanted to keep it forever.

As her teacher talked, Wonder Woman admired her mass of blond hair and the Liberty Bell emblem on her sweater.

"It is with great delight that I welcome Wonder Woman into my classroom," Liberty Belle was saying. Her voice rang loud and clear. "In honor of your being here, I've got a special lesson plan for today!"

Wonder Woman took in a sharp breath when she saw whose picture was projected on the screen in the front of the room.

"Hippolyta is the celebrated Queen of the Amazons," Liberty Belle said, placing her hands over her heart and adding, "and a personal favorite historical figure in my eyes. As legend has it, she rules over an island populated by female warriors, and has one daughter. Wonder Woman, please stand."

There were pockets of applause, most enthusiastically from her corner of the room.

"I am your mother's biggest fan," Liberty Belle gushed,

"and have read all the myths and legends ever written about her!"

As her teacher continued to sing her mother's praises, Wonder Woman began to doubt that she could ever live up to the Amazon queen's legacy. Growing up, Wonder Woman had always thought that her mother was the greatest person in the universe. Smart, strong, kind, and giving. But she didn't realize that everyone else felt the same way—and expected Wonder Woman to be just like her mom. That was asking a lot. Maybe too much.

As Liberty Belle continued, the only person not taking notes was Wonder Woman. She didn't need to. She looked down at her notepad and was surprised to find another folded piece of paper on it. She smiled. Another drawing of her and her friends, she hoped.

It wasn't.

Inside, in block lettering, a note read:

Crash much? I'll bet your mother never did when she was flying.

Wonder Woman looked around the room. Everyone was facing forward, looking at the teacher. Everyone but Cheetah—who was looking straight at her.

CHAPTER 8

After class, Cheetah was at her locker when Wonder Woman and Katana walked by.

"Wonder *Woman*?" Cheetah said too loudly. "Isn't calling yourself a woman a bit premature?"

Katana pivoted. "Chill out, Cheetah," she said in a low and menacing tone.

"*You* chill out, Katana," Cheetah purred.

They glared at each other. Neither was going to back off. Both were ready to pounce.

Wonder Woman slipped between them. "Time for our next class!" she said brightly, pulling Katana away.

Cheetah smirked.

Katana's glare was as sharp as her sword. "She's not to be trusted," she said as Wonder Woman hurried her down the hall. "My grandmother always said to listen to your instinct, and my instinct tells me that Cheetah is bad news."

"Are you close to your grandmother?" Wonder Woman

asked. She had never known her own grandmother, and her mother never spoke of her.

Katana's eyes grew soft. She nodded. Suddenly, instead of looking like an awesome Asian warrior, Katana looked lost. "I was close to her," she said, nodding again. "She was the one who convinced my parents to let me come here. My grandmother was the first female samurai super hero. I hope to be the second." She paused. "Sobo died in battle, singlehandedly fighting the army of an evil warlord who had been ravaging our hometown." Then Katana pulled her shoulders back and shook off her sad memories. "I'm here to honor her." She sighed, and then confided, "but I don't know if I can live up to my grandmother's legacy."

Wonder Woman nodded. She knew how it felt to have to live up to a legend.

That night in the dining hall, the kitchen workers were beaming. "You've got fans here," Parasite said as he mopped up a container of tapioca pudding that had splattered on the floor. No one had ever told them how much they loved their food. But Wonder Woman truly loved the chicken cubes with thick gravy lumped over toast. It was unique. And Jell-O? "Hello, Jell-O!" she kept saying when she poked it. Who knew that food could be so fun—or so wiggly?

As Wonder Woman carried her tray and weaved in and out

of the tables and other students, she almost collided with Star Sapphire again.

"Sorry!" Wonder Woman said, raising her tray high in the air to avoid a crash. She looked at Star Sapphire's ring. "Pretty," she said, unable to stop staring at it.

"It was a gift from the Violet Lanterns," Star Sapphire told her.

"That was nice of them!" Wonder Woman said.

"I know," said Star Sapphire as she motioned Golden Glider over.

"That's dazzling, too," Wonder Woman said, pointing to the brooch Golden Glider wore on her right shoulder.

"Live?" Wonder Woman asked, still looking at Golden Glider's pin. "Does it stand for anything, or is it just, you know, 'Live!'?"

"Who can say?" Golden Glider said, shrugging and skating away with Star Sapphire.

Wonder Woman was perplexed. She said, "Where can I find this 'who'?"—but the two were all the way across the dining hall.

"It's because she's a Violet Lantern," Katana explained later. She threw a sheet of paper into the air, sliced it up with her sword, and handed Wonder Woman a string of paper super heroes. "Star Sapphire's got that ring. It makes you like her."

"Please pass the popcorn," Bumblebee said. She poured more into her bowl and then drizzled honey over it. For someone who could get so small, she had a big appetite.

Wonder Woman's friends had all gathered in her room. Some were sitting on her bed, others were on Harley's, and every now and then someone would stretch out and float in the air.

"Cookie?" Hawkgirl asked, opening a tin of home-baked chocolate chocolate chip cookies that her Abuela Muñoz had sent in her weekly care package.

"My grandmother used to bake between battles," Katana said.

"My *abuela* was a stay-at-home hero," Hawkgirl said.

Wonder Woman took a bite. The cookie was crispy on the outside and chewy on the inside, and buttery through and through.

"She put her heroing duties aside and has raised me on her own since I was a baby," Hawkgirl continued.

There was an awkward silence. No one asked what had happened to Hawkgirl's parents. At Super Hero High School, there seemed to be an unusually high number of dead parents. Occupational hazard.

"I'm so sorry," Wonder Woman said. The mere thought of losing her mother made her blink back tears. "Does it hurt?"

"Of course it hurts," Katana snapped. Wonder Woman remembered that Katana had lost her beloved grandmother in battle. "But it makes what we do all the more serious. We know the risks, unlike some wannabes. Being a super hero isn't just fun and games. It can be life or death."

"Let's remember why we're here!" Bumblebee said brightly, attempting to sweep away the gloom that threatened to ruin the day. "We all agreed to help come up with a nickname for Wonder Woman."

Wonder Woman had asked for suggestions. Sure, Cheetah had probably just been trying to rile her up when she'd made fun of her name. Still, it got Wonder Woman thinking about the possibilities.

"Where I come from, there's no difference between a girl and a woman," Wonder Woman tried to explain. "Every girl is a woman, and every woman is a girl. But a nickname would be pretty cool!"

With the cookies almost gone, the brainstorming began in earnest. Everyone had ideas. . . .

Bumblebee: "WoWo?"

Katana: "Double-Double-You?"

Hawkgirl: "Amazombie?"

Poison Ivy: "Wonderama?"

As they continued to throw out suggestions, the door was flung open and Harley rushed in.

"Hey, all! Gotta go!" she called, after grabbing the last cookie and her camera. "Don't say anything fascinating unless I'm there to video it!" And then she was gone.

Katana was about to speak when Harley leapt back in the room. "Wondy! We should call her Wondy!" she called before disappearing again.

There was a silence while everyone mulled it over.

"*Wondy?* Wondy! I like that," Wonder Woman finally said. As the girls chanted "Wondy! Wondy! Wondy!" it started to sound better and better.

"Looks like you have a nickname," Katana told her.

"Thanks to all of you. And especially Harley," Wonder Woman—Wondy—said, feeling like she really belonged.

Later, after the girls left, Harley came back and put her camera down. "I had heard a rumor that some of the Supers were going to move the Amethyst Tower just for fun. But apparently that was just a rumor," Harley said, sounding disappointed. "Did you decide on your nickname?"

"Wondy!" Wonder Woman replied.

Harley lit up. "That's the one I came up with!"

Wonder Woman nodded.

"Great!" Harley shouted, bouncing off the walls. "I've got another exclusive for HQTV. I'll interview both of us! Yes! I'm building the biggest video empire in the world, and you're a part of it, Wondy!"

"Do I have to be?" Wonder Woman asked. "I mean, do you really need me?"

"Of course I do," Harley said. "Don't worry—I'd never leave you out."

"Oh, okay," Wonder Woman said. She didn't want to upset her roommate's plans for world media domination.

That night, despite the comfort of her pillow, Wonder Woman had trouble falling asleep. She had read about how quickly Harley's video channel was growing. Lois Lane's *Super News* did a whole story on it. Now that Harley was about to go all out on HQTV, Wonder Woman knew the pressure on her would be even greater, with the whole world weighing in on her every move.

What if she wasn't up to it? What if she let people down?

CHAPTER 9

Yesterday she'd woken up as Wonder Woman. Today she woke up as Wondy. Thanks to Harley's "exclusive," everyone at Super Hero High and beyond already knew about Wondy's new name. When she logged in to her email, her mother had written, *Wondy? At first I wasn't sure about the new moniker, but the more I think about it, the more I like it. You are carving out your own identity at Super Hero High. I will support it.*

Daughter, the email continued, *may I tell you a secret? When I was your age, my friends called me Lyta.*

Lyta. Wonder Woman said it aloud: "Lyta." It was so beautiful, like her mother.

Wonder Woman emailed back to thank her for understanding. She left out the expectations everyone had for her as the only daughter of "Lyta," Queen of the Amazons. She didn't want her mom to worry.

A vibrant palette of color swept into Intro to Super Suits. Wonder Woman gasped at the spectacularness of it all. The teacher was draped in a brightly colored ensemble—European-cut slacks, a multicolored patchwork vest, an outrageously purple shirt with matching ascot and a pair of glasses with—impossibly—lenses that were three different colors. Wonder Woman was particularly entranced by his hair. It looked fake, like he was wearing a helmet. *Maybe he is,* she thought. How clever! Using one's hair as a shield.

Katana, whose sleek long hair was casually draped over one shoulder, nudged her. "You're gawking," she whispered.

Wonder Woman closed her mouth and sat back down.

"Welcome, Wonder Woman," the teacher said. "I am known to the world at large as Crazy Quilt! Yes, *that* Crazy Quilt!" He struck a pose to give the class time to admire his outfit. As they did, Crazy Quilt looked around the room, shaking his head until he got to Star Sapphire, who was wearing an elegant violet smock over silver leggings and custom-made silver glitter high-tops. Crazy Quilt nodded appreciatively. "Not bad," he said to Star Sapphire. "Not bad. Not good, but not bad. Bad, yes. Good, yes. I'd say good-bad. Yes, I've come up with a new phrase—good-bad!"

Wonder Woman wrote *good-bad* in her notebook.

"Wonder Woman, the other students have already created

their own iconic super hero costumes, so you have some catching up to do. As I have told the class, your style is your first impression. It's not just look, but function—super hero function—that's graded. Plus, accessories are important. They can make or break a super hero. You may find this impossible to believe, but I wasn't always the fashion maven that I am now. So as I look around the room, I think, yes! There is hope for all of you." He paused, then added sadly, "Some more than others.

"My shoes can hide any number of weapons," Crazy Quilt continued as he bent over to retrieve a mini-blaster from the sole of his shoe. When he fell over, several students snickered. "Therefore," Crazy Quilt said, jumping back up and pretending nothing had happened, "as you can all see, fashion and function can work together for your super hero costumes!

He applauded himself and then announced, "Now let's get started, shall we? Super heroes, continue with your costumes—make sure they pass the fire, water, weather test. Wonder Woman, teams have already been selected, but I'm putting you with Star Sapphire and Golden Glider. They will assist you, giving you input and creative criticism. At the end of two months, everyone will model their own costume. The top grade will receive the coveted Crazy Quilt Award!"

Wonder Woman smiled and waved at Star Sapphire, who always looked like she had stepped off the pages of *Super Hero Supermodel* magazine—from her sleek, sparkly clothes to the way she carried herself. Star Sapphire gave an almost imperceptible nod to acknowledge her.

"Welcome to our team," Golden Glider said as she executed a perfect pirouette, stopping inches away from Wonder Woman. "We want to win, so just make sure you don't mess up, okay?"

"Okay," Wonder Woman said. She had no intention of messing up.

As Crazy Quilt circled the room talking about the dangers of ice storms versus dust storms versus moth storms on costumes, Wonder Woman surveyed the other teams. Katana and Hawkgirl sat side by side. Wonder Woman noted that Hawkgirl's clothes were as conservative as Katana's were modern and daring. Bumblebee and Cyborg were chatting happily, unlike Cheetah and Harley, who both were trying to talk at the same time. Meanwhile, Green Lantern and Frost were busy ignoring each other.

"All eyes on me!" Crazy Quilt cried as he showed Super Hero Dos and Don'ts on the screen. Wonder Woman took notes and photos.

"Your style speaks volumes," he said. "You either have it or you don't."

Cheetah leaned toward Star Sapphire and said, "And clearly our partners don't have it!"

As the two laughed, Wonder Woman wrote on her to-do list, *Get it.* "Unlike other schools," Crazy Quilt was explaining, "Super Hero High prides itself on encouraging its students' freedom of expression. Not only is it okay to mix it up and wear your super hero top with jeans and a mask, it is encouraged! Capes are the current trend for flyers and nonflyers alike. Last year, masks were all the rage, and the year before that, you couldn't even find a decent pair of laser-deflecting gloves, they were so popular," he informed them.

Having worn a skort most of her life, Wonder Woman wondered if they would ever be in style. They were the height of comfort, but perhaps pants would be a nice change. And boots. With boots you could avoid some of the pitfalls of sandals, like getting a rock stuck in them. Plus boots would be better for kicking down doors and disabling enemies!

Yes, a total costume makeover was in order, she decided.

That night, as Harley practiced backflips and sidewinders, Wonder Woman was busy wielding the sword she had borrowed from Katana. She had to make up for lost time. *How hard can it be to create a costume?* Wonder Woman thought. She had studied those videos that promised, "In three easy steps, you, too, can create an outfit that will be the envy of all your friends!"

With great enthusiasm, Wonder Woman began slashing the cloth she had brought from class. She stood back and looked at the material in front of her. Satisfied, she lassoed something from across the room, barely missing Harley, who, of course, was videoing her with interest. Wonder Woman opened the sewing kit and took out some long, deadly-looking needles. "And all I have to do is sew the pieces together!" she explained.

Harley put her camera down. "What is that?" she asked.

"Preliminary ideas are due tomorrow for Crazy Quilt's class, but I thought I'd take some material and actually try out a few things. What do you think?" Wonder Woman proudly held up her costume.

Harley squinted and blinked. "No words can describe that," she said truthfully.

Wonder Woman let out a big, happy sigh. "Thanks, Harley! I was worried that it looked funny."

The next day, Wonder Woman couldn't wait to get to Crazy Quilt's class. She had left her makeshift costume in her room, but came armed with pages and pages of sketches based on her design. Katana was working on fireproofing her costume, and in her notebook were only three drawings. They all looked the same to Wonder Woman.

Star Sapphire refused to let Wonder Woman see what she had done. "The element of surprise is best for this kind of fashion," she said. Golden Glider stood behind her, nodding.

Wonder Woman nodded, too. It was so nice to be part of a team. Her mother had always told her that the element of surprise was best for battle. She hadn't realized it was the same for clothes.

Crazy Quilt clapped his hands together. "I am hoping we'll see some groovy designs today!" he exclaimed. "When I was your age, we wore tie-dyed shirts, fringe vests, headbands, and sandals. I can't wait to see what you have to show me."

Hawkgirl and Katana went first. Holding up a pencil sketch, Hawkgirl showed a simple one-piece costume.

"What do you think of your partner's design, Katana?" the teacher asked.

"It's very functional. Aerodynamic. There's not a lot of flair, but that's in keeping with Hawkgirl's under-the-radar style. Great job!"

Crazy Quilt nodded. "Yes, yes, to go understated is a bold move. Bold move! One that I've never had the nerve to make," he mused. "All righty, Katana, show us what you've got."

Katana displayed the designs from her notebook as Hawkgirl stood up and said, "Simple and sleek, and the layers of black on black make it perfect for being stealthy in the night."

"That's what I was going for!" Katana said, smiling at her partner.

Crazy Quilt pored over the sketches, nodding. "Good, bad, good-bad!" he said. "Hmmm. But soooooo much black? This is not a funeral. Well, maybe your enemy's, but not yours. Next!"

The teams went up two by two and showed their designs. After each critique, Crazy Quilt offered his expert opinion. Never had there been so much good-bad in one room. Finally, it was time for the last team to show what they had.

"Nervous?" Star Sapphire asked.

"No," Wonder Woman answered. "Are you?"

Star Sapphire smiled sweetly. "How could I be, with you as my partner?" she said.

"Don't forget me," Golden Glider said.

"Right. You too," Star Sapphire replied, offering both a warm smile.

Wonder Woman smiled back. School was even more fun than catching comets!

CHAPTER 10

Between Crazy Quilt's observations and frequent reminiscences, the other pairs had managed to find something nice to say about each other. Even Cheetah admitted that the sketch of Harley's blue shorts and red-and-black leggings was "not awful."

At last it was Wonder Woman, Star Sapphire, and Golden Glider's turn. "You go first," Star Sapphire said generously to Wonder Woman.

"Oh! You can go first," Wonder Woman said, even though she couldn't wait to hear what her team was going to say about her design. After all, it had left Harley practically speechless, and that rarely happened.

"Yes, you go first," Golden Glider insisted to Star Sapphire.

With a flourish worthy of a runway supermodel, Star Sapphire began. While other students had held up notebooks and sketchpads with loose drawings on them, Star Sapphire had an Inspiration Board, complete with fabric samples, color charts, and professional photos of herself wearing different designs.

Wonder Woman smiled and faced the class. "It's super great! The colors! The style! The cut and the coolness factor! I think Star Sapphire should be our fashion ambassador," she said as Star Sapphire blushed.

"Pretty much perfection," Golden Glider added. "How do you do it, Star Sapphire?"

Star Sapphire shrugged as her Violet Lantern ring glowed.

Crazy Quilt leapt up to give Star Sapphire a standing ovation. "Marvelous! Groovy, cool, and hip. Good-good!"

Golden Glider was up next. Her sketches took what she was wearing up several notches, adding white glitter to her skirt, which trailed behind her as she skated, a faux-fur trim, and glistening golden highlights on the shoulders of her dress.

"Not too shabby," Star Sapphire admitted.

"So pretty! So awesome! So everything!" Wonder Woman chimed in.

Next and last was Wonder Woman. She opened her notebook and held it high above her head. Wonder Woman wished she had brought a swatch of fabric to show, like Star Sapphire had. It would have been easy enough, with all the cutting she had done with Katana's sword.

Many students turned their heads sideways to get a better view of Wonder Woman's drawing. Green Lantern rubbed his eyes and gave it a second look. Bumblebee looked surprised.

"Golden Glider, what do you think?" Crazy Quilt asked.

She looked dazzled. "It's not at all what I was expecting."

Wonder Woman mouthed, "Thank you!"

"Star Sapphire, your take on this?" Quilty said.

"I think . . . ," she began slowly. "I think it looks like someone's puppy drew this." Wonder Woman was shocked. She didn't know that dogs could draw. But Star Sapphire wasn't finished yet.

"I have to give Wonder Woman credit for trying," she said. Wonder Woman grinned. Star Sapphire still wasn't done. "This looks like a cross between a zebra, a wedding gown, and a fortress," she added.

"Thank you," Wonder Woman said, a tad confused. Did Star Sapphire just insult her design? By the horrified looks on the faces of Bumblebee, Katana, and Hawkgirl, it seemed that she had.

If she was discouraged, Wonder Woman didn't let it get to her. Instead, she tried to learn from the brutal critique, taking notes and thinking about how to improve. However, later, while many students spent their afternoon reworking their designs, Wonder Woman couldn't. She had someplace she needed to be.

From many of the school's rooftop-garden terraces, Wonder Woman had observed the goings-on in Metropolis. But this was to be her first foray into the city.

Gleaming tall, modern buildings stood next to stores run by local merchants. Cars of every size and color zipped around the streets. Some were parked crooked, while others seemed to be packed too tightly together.

As Wonder Woman was rearranging the parked cars, a flustered woman rushed out of Pinky's Nail Salon. "Wait! That's mine," she said, waving her fingers in the air, her nails freshly polished with a shade called Peachy Keen.

"Your car is so cute, it looks like a beetle," Wonder Woman said as she set it down. "I was just tidying up."

The woman looked down the street. All the cars were now parked in a straight line and evenly spaced.

"Wow, it looks great! Thank you, Wonder Woman," she said.

"You know my name?" Wonder Woman asked, surprised.

"Well, yes. Everyone knows who you are," the woman told her. "Since you arrived at Super Hero High, we've been watching you on HQTV! I'm a W-three!"

"Nice to meet you," Wonder Woman said, shaking the woman's hand and being extra careful not to break any of her bones. That would have been rude.

As Wonder Woman continued toward the Capes & Cowls Cafe, she heard, "Help!" She immediately ran toward the cries.

A woman and her little girl were outside Donut Delite, where a sign shaped like giant donut hung over the door. A tough-looking character was just about to grab the child's bag of donuts. He had already taken the woman's money and phone.

"Stop, right now!" Wonder Woman called.

The man pointed a gun at her.

"Don't do it," she warned.

"Don't do this?" he sneered, and he pulled the trigger!

Wonder Woman stood her ground as the bullet ricocheted off one of her bracelets and severed the cord that held the giant donut sign. The thief looked up as the sign fell and landed on him, the huge donut encircling him, pinning his arms to his sides.

Wonder Woman picked up the bag of donuts and returned them to the little girl.

"You're Wonder Woman!" the girl said, awestruck.

Wonder Woman smiled at the girl as she gave the woman her money and phone back. "You might want to call the police," she said.

By the time Wonder Woman made it to the Capes & Cowls Cafe, she was almost two and a half minutes late. Rushing in, she apologized to Lois Lane.

"Not a problem," Lois assured her. "You were busy doling out justice and donuts."

"How do you know?" Wonder Woman asked, surprised. Bumblebee had told her that Lois Lane was a great reporter, but this was incredible. It wasn't like Lois could read minds. She was a regular girl without superpowers. Wasn't she?

"Look," Lois said, pointing to the television.

A little girl clutching a bag of donuts was saying, "When I get bigger, I want to be just like Wonder Woman!"

"Thanks for meeting me," Lois said as Wonder Woman looked around. The cafe was cozy and quaint while still being impossibly hip, with splashy comic-book-like murals, cushy couches, and old-fashioned board games spread out on the coffee tables.

"Wondy, call me Wondy," she said, turning back to Lois Lane. "It's my new nickname!"

Lois lit up. "I can't wait to write about this," she said. "Would you mind if I asked you some questions? Everyone wants to know about Wonder Woman . . . er, Wondy."

As the two began to talk, it seemed that Wonder Woman had as many questions for Lois as Lois had for her.

"I specialize in writing profiles of up-and-coming super heroes, and with Super Hero High being so close, it's easy," Lois explained. "Plus CAD Academy is in the next town over. But what I really love doing," Lois confided, "is investigative reporting. You know, unraveling mysteries."

Wonder Woman thought it over. Lois loved solving mysteries, and Wonder Woman had one. "I'm not sure if you'd be interested in this, but it seems that someone's not too happy with me being at Super Hero High," Wonder Woman confessed.

Lois Lane perked up. "Really?" she asked, opening her reporter's notebook. "Tell me more."

Just then, a skinny boy with a messy blond hair stopped

by. "Hi, Lois!" He had a pencil tucked behind his ear. *A secret weapon, perhaps,* Wonder Woman thought. *How clever.*

"What can I get for the two of you?" he asked, offering a shy smile.

Wonder Woman stared. He didn't look as strong as Cyborg, or as fast as The Flash, but there was something about him that she liked.

"What kind of weapon is that?" she asked, pointing to the metal on his teeth.

"Huh? Oh," he said, blushing. "It's not a weapon. They're braces. You know, 'cause my teeth are crooked." He covered his mouth with his hand as he spoke.

"I like them," Wonder Woman said. "Braces. They look good on you! Maybe I'll get some."

The boy stared at Wonder Woman.

"I'll have my usual," Lois said, not bothering with the menu. "An acai berry smoothie."

Wonder Woman noticed that her heart was beating a little faster than usual. "I'll have three bowls of cereal, please," she said to the boy. "The green and blue ones shaped like crescent moons, the yellow and red ones shaped like asteroids, and the purple and pink ones shaped like flowers."

The boy shook his head apologetically. "I'm sorry, but we don't have sugar cereal here. Only healthy food. How about a veggie burger and kale chips?"

Wonder Woman nodded. "Okay, then. Those."

"Oh! Where are my manners?" Lois chided herself. "Wondy, this is Steve Trevor. His dad owns the diner. Steve, this is Wonder Woman, but she goes by Wondy now. She's new to Super Hero High."

Steve wiped his right hand on his apron and extended it. Wonder Woman made sure not to crush him when they shook hands.

"I'll get your order right away," he said, flexing his fingers as he ran off.

"He wants to be a pilot," Lois later told her new friend. "I've known him since we were little, and all he's ever wanted to do was fly."

Wonder Woman understood. "I remember when I first started to fly," she said. She noticed that Steve was now wiping and rewiping the table behind her, even though it was clean. "Sure, there were lots of crashes," Wonder Woman continued, "but my mom was always nearby in case I needed her. When I finally got good enough to fly solo—the sensation of soaring through the air, dipping in and out of clouds . . ."

Wonder Woman was interrupted by the crash of a chutney bottle. She turned around and Steve was standing there, looking at the mess.

"Er, I must have been distracted," he said.

Lois smiled knowingly. "Don't forget our order, Steve."

"Sure thing!" he said. "Let me just clean this up first."

Now it was Wonder Woman's turn to smile. She liked it when people were tidy.

"So, then, you had started telling me about a mystery," Lois reminded her.

"Right!" Wonder Woman said. "I keep getting these messages telling me I'm not wanted at Super Hero High."

"Who's sending them?" Lois asked.

"That's the mystery!" Wonder Woman exclaimed. "I'm thinking maybe it's Mandy Bowin. She's the girl who was expelled right before I showed up."

As the two discussed the matter, Wonder Woman kept her eye on Steve Trevor. He was now at the counter, struggling to open a jar of jam. In a heartbeat, she was next to him. "Can I help?" she asked.

Steve blinked back his surprise. "Uh, sure," he said handing the jar over. Wonder Woman opened it with ease. "Wow, thank you," he said, "You're really strong."

"Yes, that's true," she answered.

He was looking at her funny.

"Are you sick?" she asked.

He shook his head, but he didn't speak or take his eyes off her.

"Are you okay?" she asked.

He nodded, and he opened his mouth to say something, but nothing came out.

"Maybe your braces are broken," Wonder Woman suggested.

As she stared back at Steve, Wonder Woman started

feeling strange. *Perhaps he is sick,* she thought, *and I have caught whatever he has!*

Back in their dorm room that night, Harley said, "The more the world sees you, the more popular you become. The more popular you become, the more the world sees you!"

"Is that a good thing?" Wonder Woman asked.

"You're so funny!" Harley said, letting out one of her famous laughs.

Wonder Woman gave a weak smile, wondering what funny thing had she said this time. "Hey, Harley," she asked. "Can you explain something to me?"

"Sure, what?" Harley was now doing a handstand in the middle of the room.

"Boys," Wonder Woman said. "Can you explain them to me?"

Harley sat next to Wonder Woman on her bed. "Wow, that's a hard one," she said. "They're just like us, but not at all like us. Sometimes they like us, and sometimes they don't like us, and sometimes they just like each other, but other times they like everyone, and no two boys are alike. Boy—oh, boy. Boys!"

As Harley continued talking about boys in general, Wonder Woman continued thinking about one boy in particular.

PART TWO

CHAPTER 11

Lois Lane's interview with Metropolis's newest super hero was a smash success. Not only was it front-page news in Metropolis High's newspaper and online at *Super News,* but the *Daily Planet* picked it up and ran it in the *What's New News* section.

"Look at the famous Wonder Woman," Cheetah said as she slammed her locker shut.

"No, it's not Wonder Woman, it's *Wondy,*" Frost said, passing by. "Don't you watch HQTV?"

"You can call me either," Wonder Woman said helpfully. But by then they were gone.

Wonder Woman had heard a whiff of a nasty rumor that she wasn't living up to her press, that she had somehow tricked Lois Lane into writing the glowing article. Most of the students who believed the article were classmates of Wonder Woman's, and several, like Beast Boy, were quick to tell her how much they liked reading about her. Others remembered that she'd helped the kitchen staff. And still others benefited from the after-school tutoring sessions she had set up. Many noted that Wonder Woman was always ready with a kind word.

The following week, Harley skipped dinner again to work on her videos. Wonder Woman had gotten into the habit of bringing her a sandwich from the dining hall. Through a mouthful of food, Harley stared at the computer screen and then began to chortle. Or maybe she was choking.

"Are you okay?" Wonder Woman asked, poised to break into laughter or deliver the Heimlich maneuver, whichever was appropriate.

"I'm just cracking myself up," Harley said, wiping the tears off her face and pointing to the screen.

"May I see?" Wonder Woman asked, relieved that she didn't need to save her roommate's life. There was enough of that sort of thing during class, even though most of it was just practice.

"Why not?" Harley said grandly. "After all, you're in it!"

"I am?" Wonder Woman asked. She wondered what she would see herself doing this time.

"It's a tribute," Harley explained as Wonder Woman watched wide-eyed, "of all the most popular Super Hero High kids messing up. I'm doing this for fun!"

There was Cheetah taking an unattractive tumble and then trying to pretend it was on purpose. Poison Ivy mixing chemicals and exploding a room, again. The Riddler hitting a wall after forgetting a punch line. Katana kicking Frost's locker and getting her foot stuck in it. Golden Glider accidentally turning the swimming pool into an ice-skating rink, just as Beast Boy leapt off the diving board. Beast Boy turning into a crow right before hitting the ice, and swooping back up in the air. No one was immune to Harley's camera.

Word spread quickly down the hallway, and before a girl could yell, "That's me!" other girls had filtered into Harley and Wonder Woman's dorm room. It had gotten so cramped that some had to resort to hovering above the crowd to see the computer. But everyone had one thing in common . . . their jaws were hanging open. Though Harley was pleased, the onlookers were not. No one looked good in this video. No one but Harley, who had inserted clips of herself smiling and shouting, "HQTV!"

"It's all in the editing," Harley explained to the packed room. She had to jump up and down on her bed so everyone could see her. "I can take a regular shot of someone and then zoom in on their nostrils, and instantly they look funny. And this tribute reel highlights the bloopers and blunders everyone has made!"

Wonder Woman held her breath when her section came on. It had the title "Classics." Of course there was the time Star Sapphire dressed her down in Crazy Quilt's class—with an extreme close-up of Wonder Woman looking like she was trying not to cry. But there was new material, too. Like her dancing awkwardly when she thought no one was looking. Or mooning over a newspaper photo of Steve Trevor receiving an award for his efforts to feed the poor. However, the worst segment was in the last part of her section. It was footage of Wonder Woman's horrible stint in Flyers' Ed, where she'd landed on her rear end—causing her to emit a loud "YIKES!"

When the video ended, there was a stunned silence.

"Well?" Harley asked. "Anyone have anything to say?"

The laughter started low and began to build. Everyone turned to see who it was coming from.

Wonder Woman?

It was a loud, joyous laugh, and it cut through the seriousness that had been building inside her. Sure, she looked bad in the video, but Wonder Woman realized that if she didn't laugh at herself, no one else could.

"We look ridiculous," she said, laughing so loud that she let out a snort. Soon everyone was laughing and snorting with her. "Thanks for sharing this with us, Harley. And thanks for not posting it on HQTV."

"What do you mean?" Harley asked.

"What do *you* mean?" Wonder Woman said, her voice beginning to falter.

"It was uploading while you were watching," Harley said. "My *Tribute* video's gone live. Look, it's already got 3,417 hits!"

Wonder Woman plopped onto the bed as the others continued to laugh. What if her mother saw the video? She would question whether Wonder Woman was taking school seriously. What if she even got expelled, like Mandy Bowin?

As the visitors filed out, Hawkgirl pushed her way in. "Wondy! Wondy!" she called, clearly upset. "Did you see it?"

"Unfortunately, I did," Wondy said. "I looked and acted awful!"

"No, I mean *me*," Hawkgirl said. "Sleeping in class? I could lose my scholarship! Plus, if Abuela Muñoz sees that, she'll be so disappointed. She's old and her heart is weak, and she's not supposed to have too much excitement."

"Try to calm down," Wonder Woman told her friend. "Does your grandmother watch a lot of videos?"

Hawkgirl shook her head, "No, not really. She's not that into modern media."

"Well, there you go," Wonder Woman said. "And I heard that Principal Waller tries not to watch HQTV or the other clips of us that float around on the Internet."

Hawkgirl let out a huge sigh of relief. "Thank you, Wondy," she said. "You really are amazing."

Wonder Woman smiled on the outside, but inside, her stomach was in knots. Unlike Hawkgirl's *abuela,* Hippolyta— Queen of the Amazons, mother to Princess Wonder Woman— was definitely an HQTV subscriber.

★

When Wonder Woman checked her emails and HQTV comments the next morning, most of the WWWs said that her flaws only made them love her more. However, there were a few messages from others claiming she wasn't a super hero at all, or super, or a hero. Several adult super heroes felt the need to chime in about the proper way to break a fall. And then there was one from aNOnymoUs: *So many stumbles in so short a time? Best you leave now before someone gets expelled.*

Expelled? Though shaken, Wondy remembered to forward the threat to Lois Lane, who was collecting evidence. The only upside of the whole morning was that there was no lecturing email from Hippolyta. Maybe she hadn't seen it after all.

Wonder Woman found herself looking up her own name on the computer. She was reluctant to admit it even to herself, but she did a daily sweep of what people were saying about her. Most of it was positive, and this made her happy. When she saw what the haters had to say, Wonder Woman let herself get depressed for about three seconds. Then she tried extra hard in school so that someday she could save the world and silence the trolls.

The popular *Super Hero Hotline* show had a segment on her. Two TV analysts, both claiming to be famous former child super heroes, were debating whether the display of antics featured in Harley's *Tribute* video was a teaching moment.

"Is Wonder Woman truly an example of a teen super hero, or is she already a teen super hero has-been?" the female analyst asked as she patted her poufy hair.

"She doesn't seem ready to save the world," the male analyst added. He had no hair to pouf, but his mustache was styled in a daring upward swoop. *"And 'yikes'? What kind of word is that? Do super heroes even say that?"*

"YIKES!"

"YIKES!"

Both analysts seemed to delight in repeating "YIKES!" over and over again.

Yikes.

Wonder Woman shut her computer off. She had seen enough.

"Can you believe all the press? I'm famous!" Harley gushed as she ran into the room. "Look at this," she said, holding up a newspaper. "Lois Lane wrote an editorial saying that it's empowering for mortal teens to see their heroes mess up!" Harley paused. "What? What's the matter?"

Wonder Woman shook her head. "I don't want to be famous," she said softly.

Harley furrowed her brow. "Why not? Everyone wants fame!"

"Not me," Wonder Woman said. "I just want to be the best super hero I can be."

"And super heroes are famous," Harley insisted. "It's part of our job. We're not like the Secret Spy Guild. We're out there protecting the world, letting them know we're here for them. The more people see of us, the safer they feel. Here, read this." Harley handed her a newspaper. It was Lois's article.

> Young super heroes today are under so much pressure to succeed. To get into the right schools. To pass their super hero exams, and to perform. Let us not forget that students like the ones in Harley Quinn's HQTV Tribute video are still just kids. And what do kids do? They goof off. They mess up. They are still acting like themselves, not a glorified version of what the public wants them to be.
>
> The HQTV Tribute video did everyone a favor. It showed kids being kids—even though these happened to be super heroes-in-training. And it gave the world a glimpse of reality, empowering and encouraging mortal teens to be themselves, like the super heroes they worship. Mistakes and mess-ups happen, but let it happen here. Let it happen now. Let's not chide these super hero students who might someday save our lives. Instead let's embrace them, goofs and all.

The article made so much sense. Wonder Woman felt a wave of relief wash over her. Maybe Harley's video was a good thing after all.

Just then, Katana leapt into the room. "Wondy!" she said, out of breath. "Your mother is on campus!"

Wonder Woman stood up. Panic engulfed her. Her mother was at Super Hero High? This could not be good.

Bumblebee buzzed in. "Wondy," she said, exchanging worried glances with Katana, "The Wall wants you in her office ASAP!"

As Wonder Woman made her way to the principal's office, she could hear the talk.

"I saw her! Hippolyta is so regal!"

"Wonder Woman's mother is my hero."

"Just being near her was a thrill."

"Wondy, your mommy is here."

Huh? Wonder Woman looked up. "Hope you've been a good girl," Frost said.

"Yes, I know, thank you," Wonder Woman said, warding off the chill.

"Just trying to be helpful," Frost said, offering a phony smile.

As Wonder Woman continued down the hallway, she saw a tornado heading her way. She stepped aside, but it stopped in front of her and her Flyers' Ed teacher appeared.

"Wonder Woman," Red Tornado said, adjusting his cape. "Your mother is here."

"That's what people keep telling me," she said.

"Well, maybe you could put in a good word for me," he said. "Ask her if she remembers me from that Super Summit

CLXXVII conference, called Flight 'n' Fight, in Florida so long ago. Tell her that I was the one who gave her the red roses."

Wonder Woman had her mind on other things. Like how upset her mother would be. "Sure thing," she told her teacher.

"Thank you!" Red Tornado said. "And ask her if she'd like to have a cup of coffee, or a snack, or a meal, or whatever. I'd be happy to join her!"

Roses. Coffee. Snack. Meal. Whatever. Wonder Woman tried to remember this as she approached Principal Waller's office, but she had much more on her mind. Even before she opened the door, she felt the presence of Hippolyta, Queen of the Amazon, ruler of Paradise Island, legendary warrior. Her mother.

CHAPTER 12

"Daughter," Hippolyta said. Concern crossed her face.

"Mother," Wonder Woman answered, her head bowed.

"You may use my office for privacy," Principal Waller said. "I'm sure you have much to talk about."

"There is nothing I can say in there that I can't say here," Hippolyta told her.

Wonder Woman's eyelashes fluttered nervously as she met The Wall's eyes. For the first time, she noticed that they looked kind.

"Principal Waller, I want to thank you for taking in my daughter these past few weeks," Hippolyta began. "It pains me to say this, but from the most recent video, it's become clear that she does not belong here."

Wonder Woman gasped. Her heart sank. She opened her mouth to protest, but no sound came out. She loved Super Hero High. Sure, there had been some rough moments, but it had also been the best time of her life. She had made great friends—Katana, Bumblebee, Poison Ivy, Hawkgirl, and the rest. Her classes had taught her more than she could ever imagine. She had learned new flying and fighting skills, but there was more. Wonder Woman had come to understand that in the battle of good versus evil, going solo was always the last option. Having friends and associates you could count on made rescues and saves so much easier—and more fun.

Yes, her time at Super Hero High had been perfect. Well, almost. Okay, there were the jokes that Harley played on her to get a reaction for HQTV. And then there were those threats and unsigned messages. She had been getting more and more of them lately. Her mother didn't need to know about that.

"With all due respect, I do belong here, Mother," Wonder Woman said. "Please—let me stay."

"I've seen my share of HQTV videos," Hippolyta noted. "Instead of acting like an Amazon princess, you come off looking, well, dare I say it? Silly. Yes, silly. Wonder Woman, you are supposed to be the Ambassador for Paradise Island. And this last video?"

Principal Waller stepped forward and started to speak, but Wonder Woman jumped in first. "The classes and training here at Super Hero High are amazing. One thing we are learning is to have fun with our abilities and to be ourselves. I've gained so much knowledge in a very short time. This is where I belong, Mother."

Hippolyta winced. Seeing this, Wonder Woman added,

"I will return to Paradise Island someday, I promise. But for now, I want to go to Super Hero High. I *need* to go to Super Hero High. There is a great big world outside Paradise Island, and it needs me. Mother, since I was a little girl, you have instilled in me the value of being a great hero. You have told me that it is our mission to help save the world. By being here, I am learning about that world. How can I save something I know nothing about?"

Wonder Woman could not read her mother's stoic expression.

"Please," she added softly.

Now it was Principal Waller's turn.

"Hippolyta, hijinks are normal for super heroes this age—all teenagers, in fact. Nothing Wonder Woman has done has broken any rules of the school or harmed anyone. These kids aren't that different from non-super teens, other than the fact that they are gossiped about in the press and cameras seem to always be on them."

"She said 'YIKES!'" Hippolyta reminded the principal. "She goofed off at school."

"Yes, and she's also made incredible strides as a super hero, though there are no videos of that. And if you hadn't seen Harley Quinn's HQTV, you wouldn't have known about Wonder Woman's missteps. I'm sure you participated in your share of antics when you were a teen."

Wonder Woman thought she saw her mother flinch—she couldn't believe it.

Principal Waller continued, "The main difference between then and now is that there weren't cell-phone cameras in everyone's hands to record what we were up to. I'm not saying that Wonder Woman should goof off. But what I am saying is that these kids have even more pressure on them to succeed here."

"As they should," Hippolyta said. "These teens are role models. They are the super heroes of tomorrow."

"Exactly," Principal Waller agreed. "Exactly. Of *tomorrow*. But for today, let them dance, let them make mistakes, let them be kids. We all know the pressures that will be on them once they leave Super Hero High. There will be little time for fun and frivolity. Saving the world is serious business. Won't you let Wonder Woman stay with us for a while? I promise to keep an eye on her."

The room was silent except for a slight buzzing.

Finally, Hippolyta's face softened. "I will give you another chance, Wonder Woman," her mother said, gathering her daughter in her arms. "Forgive me for doubting you. You have never been anything but true."

Wonder Woman returned her mother's hug, melting into her arms, before they let each other go and stood up straight.

Hippolyta turned to Principal Waller, "I need assurances that my daughter will be well-behaved, in accordance with her upbringing as a princess and a hero. Can you tell me what you will do to assure that?"

Principal Waller nodded. "Starting this afternoon, I will recommend that Wondy, er, Wonder Woman, see Dr. Jeremiah Arkham, our school counselor. He deals with many of our students and can be instrumental in keeping her on track. If once a week is not enough, we can bump it up to two or even three times a week. It will also give Wonder Woman an opportunity to discuss her feelings and successes and failures with a trained professional."

Hippolyta turned to Wonder Woman. "Dearest daughter, it is hard for me to let you go. You are my heart and soul. But I cannot be happy unless you are. If I have your word that you will try your best to represent Paradise Island and that you will follow Principal Waller's guidance, then you may stay."

Wonder Woman tried hard not to bounce up and down. She could stay! She could stay! She could stay!

"Yes, Mother," Wonder Woman said in the most solemn voice she could muster.

She could stay! She could stay! She could stay!

Hippolyta gave her the look. The one that said, *Wait, I'm not done yet.* "Wonder Woman, I am putting my trust in you, in Principal Waller, and in Super Hero High. Do you have anything else to say?"

Wonder Woman thought for a moment, and then brightened. "Yes! Roses. Coffee. Snack. Meal. Whatever."

★

When Wonder Woman and her mother left the principal's office, Bumblebee was in the hallway, leaning against a locker and looking guilty. She waved to Wonder Woman and quickly flew away.

After Wonder Woman walked her mother outside, they embraced. Wonder Woman did not want to let go. She wanted to cry. She had been so busy at Super Hero High that she had forgotten how much she missed her mom.

Wonder Woman stood below the Amethyst statue that had welcomed her to Super Hero High and watched her mother fly away. Nearby were Cyborg and Barbara Gordon. It looked like they were telling secrets, but then Barbara took out a screwdriver and other tools and began to tinker with Cyborg's head.

Wonder Woman turned back to the clouds, but by then her mother was gone.

"She's really amazing," someone said.

Wonder Woman was surprised to find Barbara Gordon standing next to her. Wonder Woman had noticed her around the school more and more lately. Barbara had been the one to show Wonder Woman how to access her locker, and recently The Wall had hired Barbara as the school's tech expert.

"Thanks," Wonder Woman said. "She *is* amazing."

"I was just fixing Cyborg's internal circuitry," Barbara said, sitting down on the grass. "Sometimes when he gets upset, his brain starts to misfire, and it gives him a killer headache."

"Sometimes I get headaches," Wonder Woman said, letting out a sigh.

"Really?" Barbara asked.

Wonder Woman tried to smile. "It can be hard being the daughter of a queen. So many people expect so much from you."

"Tell me about it," Barbara said. She tightened the laces on her blue sneakers. "My dad is Police Commissioner Gordon."

Wonder Woman nodded. Everyone knew who he was. He taught Forensics and Law Enforcement and You, a class Wonder Woman was looking forward to taking next semester.

"He wants me to have a job that's not dangerous," Barbara said. "Something safe, which translates to something boring."

"What do *you* want to do?" Wonder Woman asked.

Barbara's face lit up. "I want to fight crime," she said in a rush. "But I need to learn how to do that."

"Maybe you could go to school here," Wonder Woman suggested. "Principal Waller already knows you."

Barbara let out a laugh. Unlike Harley's laugh, which was loud and boisterous, hers was light and warm. "That'll be the day," Barbara said. "I'm a regular girl, not a super hero. I don't have any powers."

"You're a tech wizard," Wonder Woman pointed out.

Barbara stood up, still laughing. "You're so funny, Wonder Woman. Thanks for that!"

Wonder Woman watched Barbara Gordon walk back into the building. *She could be a super hero,* Wonder Woman thought. *Isn't Super Hero High all about potential?*

★

"What makes you think you can save the world?"

Wonder Woman squirmed in the overstuffed armchair and looked back at Dr. Arkham. His eyes were huge. He had a lot of gray hair, all of which resided on his chin in the form of a bushy beard, leaving the top of his head gloriously bald and shiny.

"It's something I've always known I can do," Wonder Woman said earnestly.

"Hmmm," Dr. Arkham replied, writing on his yellow notepad. He adjusted his heavy round glasses before asking her a battery of questions.

Wonder Woman answered as quickly and honestly as she could.

"Red."

"Cereal."

"Birds."

"Mom."

"Collywobbles."

"Itsy-bitsy."

"Steve."

"Boils."

"Karaoke."

She was exhausted by the time she was done. As Dr. Arkham scribbled on his notepad, Wonder Woman surveyed his dark, dusty office. There were several photos of him shaking hands with famous super heroes, a life-sized suit of armor, and towering piles of books everywhere. On his desk were a collection of globes, a dusty old typewriter, and a partially finished jigsaw puzzle of the human brain.

"Is there anything you'd like to talk about?" Dr. Arkham asked.

"Yes, well, I think someone is out to get me . . . ," Wonder Woman began.

"Hmmm . . . interesting," Dr. Arkham murmured. "So! Have I told you about the new book I'm writing?"

Wonder Woman nodded. He had indeed told her about *The Mind and Manners of the Adolescent Super Hero, Volume Five.* Twice.

"No? Well, it's called *The Mind and Manners of the Adolescent Super Hero, Volume Five.* You don't mind if I use some of what you've told me in it do you?"

"Um, I'd rather you not . . . ," Wonder Woman began.

"Great! Okay, yes. I'll use some quotes from you. But don't worry, I won't use your real name. We'll give you a moniker. Something catchy. How's that?"

"Well . . ."

"How about Wonderful Woman? Yes! That's it."

"It's not really what I would have picked," Wonder Woman

said. "And you're probably better off leaving me out of your books. The Amazonian lawyers are warriors. Literally. You should see the damage they can inflict with just the threat of a lawsuit."

Dr. Arkham swallowed hard. For once, it seemed that he understood what Wonder Woman was saying.

"So, Wonderfu—er, I mean, Wonder Woman, tell me why you're here."

"I've made some mistakes," she admitted. "Harley says I've been sort of a glorious goofball and a ratings bonanza, and I guess I'm a little stressed. There are so many classes and tests, and there never seems to be enough time to fit everything in. Plus there's that person who's been threatening me."

Dr. Arkham nodded and stroked his beard. There was a long silence, and then he said, "You should stop being stressed."

"Oh, okay," Wonder Woman said. Why hadn't she thought of that?

"Here," Dr. Arkham said, rising and handing her a pile of books. "You're going to love these."

Wonder Woman looked down at *The Mind and Manners of the Adolescent Super Hero,* volumes one, two, three, and four.

"Read those before our session next week, and learn how to relax. I know! How about joining some clubs? Yes! Great idea. And try yoga! *Relax,*" he said. "R-E-L-A-X!"

Before she left, Dr. Arkham stood up. They were the same height. "Wonder Woman," he said, taking off his glasses. She was surprised to see that his eyes now looked normal-sized. "You're putting too much pressure on yourself. Classic overachiever, that would be you. There will be plenty of time to save the world, but right now I want you to take care of yourself."

Wonder Woman nodded, not quite sure what he meant.

That night, as she sat on her bed surrounded by books, Wonder Woman added to her to-do list:

* *Don't stress*
* *Relax*
* *Read four volumes of* The Mind and Manners of the Adolescent Super Hero
* *Join clubs*
* *Learn yoga*

CHAPTER 13

Wonder Woman was great at most things. Relaxing was not one of them. Yoga made her tense. She struggled to get through *The Mind and Manners of the Adolescent Super Hero*, volumes one, two, three, and four, which she found stressful, especially since Dr. Arkham tended to repeat himself as much in print as he did in person. However, Wonder Woman did enjoy checking out all the clubs on campus.

She had noticed that Poison Ivy often hid in the back of the room or got quiet when the other girls where talking up a storm, so Wonder Woman invited her plant-loving pal to join her.

"Ivy, didn't you tell me that Principal Waller said you should join at least one club? I'm going look into what's out there. Plus it'll be fun finding out what interests everyone!" Wonder Woman said.

"I'm not so sure." Poison Ivy hesitated. She nervously tugged on her red hair, causing her ivy weave to go askew.

"What if they ask a lot of questions?"

"We'll be the ones asking the questions," Wonder Woman assured her. "We're just going to find out what each club is about and decide if we want to join any."

"Do we have to join them?" Poison Ivy asked. As they walked, she kept stopping to encourage trees to grow. She knew all the plants by name. "That's Katie, and she's a sunflower, and that's Benny. He's a *ficus benjamina*. . . ." She knew how to care for each one.

"We don't have to join any club we don't want to," Wonder Woman assured her friend. "And you don't have to talk at all if you don't feel like it. If you have a question, you can tell me and I'll ask for you."

Poison Ivy looked relieved.

Some Supers were sitting in trees. Others were hiding in the bushes. They were very, very quiet. Most had binoculars, though a few used their more-than-perfect vision to spot the birds.

"We meet once a week," Hawkgirl whispered as she explained the Bird-Watchers Club to Wonder Woman and Poison Ivy. "Each of us has one of these." She held up an orange notebook. "We record the birds we see."

"Like that one?" Wonder Woman said, pointing to a small pink polka-dotted bird perched on a pinecone still attached to a tree.

There was an almost silent commotion as the bird watchers trained their eyes and their binoculars in unison on the bird.

"The Spotty Dotty is so rare," Hawkgirl whispered, "that even experts have doubted its existence!"

Green Lantern handed an application to Wonder Woman. "We would be honored if you would join the Bird-Watchers Club," he said softly. "It's the best club on campus."

She cleared her throat and glanced sideways at Poison Ivy, who was standing next to her.

"Oh! And you, too, uh . . . Patty," he said.

"Poison," she corrected him. "I'm Poison Ivy. We have Weaponomics together. I sit next to you."

"Ha, ha! Yes, of course," he said, looking embarrassed. "I hope you join, too."

Wonder Woman handed over her completed application. Poison Ivy respectfully declined to join.

At the MUP Club, Starfire and Beast Boy were showing the group a floating chart of territories in the solar system.

"This is us," Starfire said, pointing to Earth.

"And this is everyone else," Beast Boy added, waving his arms in the air. "MUP stands for Model United Planets." In a conspiratorial tone, he added, "I'm the representative from Earth." He pointed to Starfire. "She's representing the Planet Tamaran."

Starfire nodded. Her intergalactic alien voice was so soft, everyone leaned forward to hear her. "Earth is not the only planet in the solar system. There are actually nine planets in total—so glad they let Pluto back in—and in the universe, there are about five hundred billion galaxies, which means there are approximately fifty sextillion habitable planets. I hope to discover some new ones one day."

"This is so exciting!" Wonder Woman exclaimed. "Will you be learning about each and every one?"

"As many as we have time for," Beast Boy assured her.

Poison Ivy poked Wonder Woman's arm. "All these clubs are overwhelming. They're making me nervous. I don't think I can handle this."

Wonder Woman handed over her completed application. Poison Ivy respectfully declined to join.

Harley Quinn could be heard before they even entered the Speech and Debate Club room. She was standing on a desk yelling at Katana, who was standing on another desk.

"You're wrong!" Harley cried.

"No, *you're* wrong!" Katana shot back.

"You don't even know what you're talking about," Harley said.

"I know more than you do!" Katana informed her.

"What's the topic?" Wonder Woman asked.

Both girls looked surprised to see her and Poison Ivy standing in the room.

"The topic?" Harley asked, doing a backflip off the desk. "Hey, Katana, what were we debating this time?"

Katana jumped down and did a kick spin. "That you were

wrong and I was right," she said, sporting a mischievous grin.

"Is it always like this?" Poison Ivy asked meekly.

Katana shook her head. "No, sometimes we get loud and angry."

"You two should join," Katana said. "Tell them, Harley."

"She's right," Harley agreed. It was hard to believe she and Katana had been arguing just minutes earlier. "We debate, and we also give speeches and compete with teams from other schools. It's fun!"

"Fun?" Poison Ivy asked.

"YES!" Katana and Harley said in unison. Poison Ivy flinched.

Wonder Woman handed over her completed application. Poison Ivy respectfully declined to join.

And so it went with every club. Wonder Woman eagerly joined, finding each club more fascinating than the one before it. When they got to the last one on their list, Poison Ivy had yet to join any.

"Science Club," Wonder Woman announced as they entered the lab.

Poison Ivy's eyes lit up when she saw the glimmering test tubes bubbling with brightly colored liquids. Most students were hunched over microscopes.

"What are you looking at?" Poison Ivy asked.

Frost sighed as if bothered. "I'm looking at you right now, interrupting me," she said, returning to her experiment. She grinned when the ordinary glass of water in front of her suddenly crystallized and grew into a sharp ice dagger.

"Sorry." Poison Ivy blinked back her surprise. "Excuse me," she said. "I was just curious."

"What kinds of things do you do in this club?" Wonder Woman asked. She peered at the petri dishes. Some were full of fuzz. Others had what looked like tiny green lumps growing in them. One had a miniature ocean in it, complete with waves and cliffs.

Poison Ivy was admiring the plants on the windowsill.

"We do all sorts of science experiments," Cyborg explained. "I've been studying the effects of lightning on the computer chip in my brain, and Frost has been trying to come up with a new freeze capsule that, when dropped into water, can create winter."

"Do you do much with plants?" Poison Ivy asked.

"All the time," Cyborg said as Wonder Woman studied him. He was a truly fascinating combination of technology and humanity. Cyborg, quite literally, was half human and half machine. Wonder Woman was having trouble figuring out which part was which.

"We all do our own experiments, set our own goals, and record our own results," Cyborg continued, oblivious to Wonder Woman's staring. "However, we exchange ideas and suggestions, and the last half hour of every club meeting is devoted to sharing what we have learned."

"May I have an application?" Poison Ivy asked, surprising Wonder Woman.

"Sure," Cyborg said. "We'd love for you to join us. What about you, Wonder Woman? Can we interest you in science?"

"We're both joining," Wonder Woman enthused. Frost handed Poison Ivy an icicle to use to sign her name. "Principal Waller will be thrilled with your choice, Ivy!"

Of the many clubs she had joined, Wonder Woman was most fond of the Science Club. She got to watch Poison Ivy blossom. Though usually quiet, Poison Ivy did not hesitate to speak up to her fellow science lovers. They shared ideas and experiments, and Wonder Woman noticed that even Star Sapphire, who was hard to impress, was taking note of Poison Ivy's savvy in the science room. Plus, no one flinched when Poison Ivy's modified interplanetary plants began to explode, causing mayhem and chaos across the school as the green plant pods rolled into the hallway like live grenades. By the end of the second week, they were used to this.

"I love it!" Harley chortled as she captured it for HQTV. "Poison Ivy," she shouted through the smoke. "Who knew that behind that quiet facade you were made for the media?"

By now, all the students were used to Harley and her video camera. Some preened when the red light was on, and others ignored it. Most just went about their business. However, Wonder Woman was being very careful, lest her mother see her behaving in a manner she wouldn't approve of. Wonder

Woman knew she had been given a second chance, and she wasn't about to blow it.

Overachiever that she was, Wonder Woman loved high school and found a way to ace her classes, attend club meetings, volunteer at the alien animal shelter, and have a social life. Her strategy was simple: she just didn't sleep. Even Dr. Arkham had to agree that Wonder Woman was doing well at Super Hero High, though he credited it to his books and their weekly sessions.

The first time Wonder Woman fell asleep while he was talking, Dr. Arkham was insulted. The second time, he fell asleep, too. The third time they both fell asleep, and it went unspoken that this was to be their routine. The benefits were instantaneous! When their hour was up, both awoke refreshed and felt better than ever.

"Well, that worked!" Dr. Arkham declared. "I think I'll write a book called *Superpower Naps: The Arkham Method,*" he added before dozing off again.

With Wonder Woman's increasingly astronomical proficiency in Flyers' Ed, most had forgotten her ill-fated first flight in class. Though her flying was not as stylish as Star Sapphire's, or as athletic as Hawkgirl's, or as acrobatic as Bumblebee's, Wonder Woman had a flair all her own. Strong and no-nonsense—no fancy flips or show-offy moves. Instead, she nailed each test with the accuracy and efficiency of an expert.

In Weaponomics, Wonder Woman proved to be a master with her with lasso, having reined in adversaries and mythological beasts since she was a toddler. Gaining control over her new deflecting bracelets took some practice. Once, when she was blocking lasers, the beams ricocheted off the bracelets and accidentally cut off the power to the school.

"Aim! Make sure your aim is accurate!" Lucius Fox yelled, jumping up and down.

The next time, under Mr. Fox's direction, Wonder Woman *purposely* shut down the school's power. Her teacher nodded in appreciation, then gave Barbara Gordon the all clear to get the school up and running again.

Heroes Throughout History proved to be endlessly fascinating. Learning about those who had helped save the world before her time often left Wonder Woman speechless and starry-eyed. Liberty Belle wove her history lessons into the most amazing true tales, and encouraged her students to share their stories as well.

Hawkgirl spoke of her parents, now deceased, and her Abuela Muñoz in Venezuela. Star Sapphire bragged about her high-achieving family. Golden Glider talked about her brother, plus a distant cousin who had discovered a previously unknown solar system. Katana honored her Japanese non–super hero parents and her Samurai super hero grandmother.

"Yes, super heroes can skip a generation," Liberty Belle

explained. "There could even be a dormant super hero gene in someone's lineage. Many people don't know their full potential until they are faced with a crisis. Conversely, just because someone has superpowers, that doesn't mean they will become a super hero."

In phys ed, Wildcat was tough on his students. He had to be. Strength and agility were important components of being a super hero. On any given day, some could be seen tossing trucks back and forth, while others were running the fifty-mile obstacle course—dodging lasers, swimming with hungry sea serpents, and bounding over a huge hill of angry termites. Meanwhile, still others sat focused on the floor as they were pelted with taunts and threats.

The last was the hardest for the Supers. For, as Wildcat explained, "It's not just physical strength that makes a stellar super hero. It's mental strength as well. You must learn to focus, to home in on your target, and to not let anyone or anything, *anything,* distract you. Self-control is your biggest challenge."

Wonder Woman excelled in all these classes. She'd even heard rumblings that she was guaranteed a spot on the Super Triathlon team. Was that the reason The Wall had recruited her?

CHAPTER 14

The only class Wonder Woman worried about was Intro to Super Suits. Though there was still time before her final costume was due, Wonder Woman had been working tirelessly, and it was almost complete. She was hoping to get extra credit for turning it in early. Wonder Woman loved extra credit—it was something they didn't have on Paradise Island.

"That is so unique," Star Sapphire said. "It's totally you!"

Wonder Woman looked up at her partner and smiled. She admired her sense of style, so to hear something like that from Star Sapphire was the ultimate compliment.

"Thank you times a billion!" Wonder Woman said.

"I've never seen anything like it," Star Sapphire added.

"No one has," Golden Glider said coolly.

"It's to die for," Cheetah purred.

"Totally," Star Sapphire added.

"Oh, Star Sapphire, thank you! You've been such an

inspiration!" Wonder Woman said, smiling widely.

Star Sapphire smiled as her violet ring glowed.

It was she who had suggested that Wonder Woman embrace the retro look. "Big jewelry. Everything big. Over-the-top big."

"I just knew we'd become friends," Wonder Woman said. "Even though some Supers say you're a snob, I never believed them! Your advice and opinions mean so much to me!"

"Thanks?" Star Sapphire said.

"I thought maybe you hated me and my designs," Wonder Woman continued. "But that's not true, is it?"

Star Sapphire gave Wonder Woman a warm smile. "I'm sorry if I was harsh on you," she said, lowering her eyes. "I'm often misunderstood."

"Oh!" Wonder Woman exclaimed, tearing up. "I'm the one who's sorry." She opened her arms for an embrace. "Friends?"

Star Sapphire gave her a huge hug. "Friends!" she said.

"Ladies, sorry to interrupt your hug fest," Crazy Quilt said, strolling over to them. His oversized multicolored sunglasses hid most of his face, and he carried his jaunty orange beret in his hands lest he fall victim to that scourge of stylish men and women the world over: hat hair. "What have we here?"

Wonder Woman smiled and pointed to the worktable. "My super hero costume," she said, glowing. "Would you like to see it?"

"In time, in time," Crazy Quilt assured her. He became

distracted by his own image in the mirror. "Time? That reminds me!"

Instead of continuing his critiques on How to Wear Your Weapons, Crazy Quilt pulled the screen down and treated the Supers to a "meticulously curated collection of my photos when I was a top student at the prestigious FISH— the Fashion Institute of Super Heroes!"

The first photo showed a youthful Crazy Quilt wearing cut-off jeans, a tie-dyed T-shirt, and lots of colorful plastic beads around his neck. He wore a green Day-Glo headband around his massive head of curly dark brown hair.

As the slide show went on and on, and on and on, featuring Crazy Quilt's greatest fashion hits through the years, Katana sidled up to Wonder Woman. "Your costume is done already?" she whispered. "That was fast. You still have over a month left before it's due."

"I couldn't wait," Wonder Woman said, lowering her voice. "Star Sapphire says she's never seen anything like it before!"

Katana squinted in the darkened room and scrutinized the outfit on the table.

"Hmmm . . . try it on," Katana whispered to Wonder Woman. "We're due for a break, and if Crazy Quilt doesn't give us one soon, we'll all die of boredom."

"Okay!" Wonder Woman said, eager to show off her creation. She had studied all the super hero costumes through the years and worked hard to bring the best of everything together.

"I am so sorry," Crazy Quilt said, turning the lights back on and waking everyone up. "But that's the end of Crazy Quilt's photos for today—as you see before you, in all its glory and grandeur, the iconic look I finally settled on." He held up his hands to ward off the applause that hadn't started yet. "We'll take a ten-minute breather and then get back to how to wear your weapons with panache!"

When Wonder Woman came out of the bathroom stall wearing her costume, Katana, who normally had a lot to say, was speechless.

"Well?" Wonder Woman said proudly. "What do you think?"

"Star Sapphire said she liked this?" Katana asked. Wonder Woman nodded. "Wondy, I think she's led you astray."

"What do you mean?" Wonder Woman asked, modeling her outfit, walking feet first, hands on her hips, a scowl on her face, as she'd seen on the hit Internet reality show *Successful Super Supermodels*.

Katana shook her head. Wonder Woman was wearing an oversized pink collar that framed her entire face—emphasizing the gigantic headpiece that replaced her usual tasteful gold tiara. It held a huge *W* on top that was so big, it threatened to wobble off. She also wore a thick, garish belt, fancy thigh-high high-heeled boots with platform soles, and long gloves that went all the way up her arms. And her voluminous magenta cape somehow made Wonder Woman look small.

"It's . . . it's . . ."

"Yes?" Wonder Woman said, ready to smile.

"It's awful," Katana blurted.

Wonder Woman's face collapsed. "Well, Star Sapphire likes it, and she's very stylish," she sputtered.

"I'm no slouch in the fashion department, either," Katana said defensively. "But I think Star Sapphire's been setting you up for an epic fail."

"No . . . no," Wonder Woman said. "Why would she do that? We're partners. We help each other."

Just then, the school began to vibrate as a loud horn blasted. "Save the day! Save the day! Save the day!" was bellowed over the loud speakers. All the students and teachers immediately streamed into the hallways and out to the courtyard.

"It's happening!" Wonder Woman shouted with delight. "Save the Day!"

"Save the Day alarm!" Bumblebee announced as Supers streamed down the hallway, running, flying, sliding, rolling. "Come on!" she said, flying and swooping in and out of the throng of students.

As the girls rushed out of building, Wonder Woman forgot she was wearing her new super hero costume. Her cape got caught in the door when it slammed, but she kept going until—*SNAP!* The cape stretched to its limit before catapulting Wonder Woman in the opposite direction. Supers ducked as Wonder Woman flew back to the doorway.

She hit the heavy metal door with a thud, but not before she had mowed down dozens of students in her wake. "Sorry! Sorry! Sorry!" Wonder Woman yelled as each one fell.

There was still time to save the day!

As she ran, the immense, stylized *W* on her headgear slid down over her eyes, blocking her vision. Still, Wonder Woman kept going, until she finally tore off the offending helmet and flung it to the side. "Sorry," she cried as Green Lantern dodged the discarded accessory. "I'm off to save the day!"

From where she was standing atop the Lady Justice statue, Wonder Woman could see someone dangling from the very pinnacle of the school—trapped near the school's iconic Amethyst. Dozens of Supers were already rising into the sky, their capes flowing in the breeze like the proud flags of many nations. Wonder Woman spotted Hawkgirl leading the charge. She would need all her speed to overtake the swarm of heroes if she was going to save the day. Wonder Woman ran toward the tower, but the grass was wet, and her high-heeled boots sank into the ground with every stride, weighing her down even more.

Up! Up! Wonder Woman realized she could go up only if she shed her clumsy boots and flew. As she looked down at the super heroes still running around, she kicked off her platform boots and was horrified when one of them knocked Poison Ivy to the ground. She was about to turn around to help her friend, but then she realized it was Mr. Fox who was hanging from the gemstone.

"Oh! Oh!" he shouted weakly. "I'm hoping some super hero will come rescue me!" He bit into a baloney sandwich and chewed. "Oh! Oh! Someone save me! Oh!"

"I'm coming," Wonder Woman called. "I'll save you, Mr. F!"

Fox continued crying as if reciting a memorized script. "Help!" He paused to mutter, "This is getting bor-ing! Anyone have some mustard? Oh, help."

Wonder Woman reached for her lasso, but it was not there. All she had was the heavy belt around her waist. At last Wonder Woman untied Mr. Fox, who was almost done with his sandwich. "Disaster. This is a disaster," he said. "It's about time someone saved me."

"Hold on to my belt," Wonder Woman said as she flew her teacher down to safety.

She had saved the day!

"That was AWFUL," The Wall bellowed. "Just awful!"

The auditorium was silent.

Wonder Woman raised her hand. "But I saved Mr. Fox," she told the principal. Perhaps The Wall was unaware of that?

All the teachers were sitting onstage, and none looked happy, especially Lucius Fox.

"By my estimations," Wildcat said, "Fox would have been done for by the time you actually got there."

"Yes," Liberty Belle added. "And regretfully, Wonder Woman, in the process of rescuing Mr. Fox, you injured several students."

Wonder Woman hung her head.

"I expect all of you to perform better during the next Save the Day drill," The Wall said sharply. "If you can't do well on an exercise, how can you expect to save the world? How would you even perform an ordinary rescue, such as an avalanche or a mutant attack?" Without waiting for an answer, she added, "Everyone, back to your classrooms, NOW. You have much to learn."

The mood back in Crazy Quilt's class was somber. As Crazy Quilt looked at Wonder Woman's outfit, he shook his head. "This is what you've been working on?" he asked.

"I had a crown and a cape and platform-stiletto boots, and . . . ," she began.

"And how did those work for you?"

"They didn't," Wonder Woman admitted, hanging her head. "They didn't work at all."

"As much as I love fashion," Crazy Quilt said, "function is just as important. Your costume is a reflection of you and must aid you in every way possible. It's not enough to look good—you must perform well. Watch."

The class went slack-jawed as their crazy teacher began to spin around, his ascot creating an orbit of power around him. Then he took off each shoe and tossed them at the window, breaking the glass and sending them out into space.

"Wait for it. . . . Wait for it. . . ." Crazy Quilt held his hands in the air as the shoes returned and he snatched each one. "They have circled the earth," he said. "And had I needed them to, they could have homed in on any enemy while my circle of power kept me safe. And that, class, is what Crazy Quilt calls fashion and function. Learn it."

That night at dinner, Wonder Woman was not her usual happy self.

"Wowza," Harley said as Wonder Woman pushed her meat loaf log and mashed potatoes around her plate. "So sorry about your costume fiasco. Although it did get high HQTV ratings. Maybe you could go back to your Amazon warrior princess clothes. You know, the outfit you came to school wearing. You could at least pass the class with that."

Passing the class was not enough, Wonder Woman knew. Her mother was expecting her to ace all her subjects, and Principal Waller was, too. Wonder Woman looked down on her tray. Another note had seemingly appeared out of nowhere. It read: *Crash and burn! You couldn't save the day and you can't save yourself. Leave now before it's too late.*

Wonder Woman crumpled up the paper and tossed it in the trash, then thought better of it. Lois Lane would want to see it, although it wasn't all that different from the other notes, emails, and comments on the HQTV website that had been showing up more and more often. Wonder Woman knew not to tell her mother about them. That would get her pulled out of school for sure.

"I've got it all on video, and it's ready to post!" Harley crowed as Wonder Woman dragged herself into her room flopped onto the bed.

"Please, Harley," she said. "Would you mind forgetting about this one? I look so foolish."

"That's the point," Harley said gleefully. "We all do! But that's why people tune in. To see super hero disasters."

Is that what I am? Wonder Woman wondered. *A super hero disaster?*

CHAPTER 15

Wonder Woman sat still. She couldn't believe she had been at Super Hero High for four weeks already. Yet here she was at another monthly assembly. Even though she knew she had no chance, she held her breath. It would be such an honor. Maybe someday . . .

Principal Waller stood tall as she looked out over the auditorium of student heroes. She stepped up to the edge of the stage and announced, "This month's Student Hero of the Month is . . . Hawkgirl!"

Wonder Woman leapt from her seat with such a burst of excitement that she hit her head on the ceiling. She fixed her hair and cheered her friend on as Harley caught Hawkgirl's surprised expression on camera and Lois Lane took notes. The lights dimmed and a video rolled, showing Hawkgirl flying over Mount Rushmore during her summer vacation. Then Hawkgirl removed the boulders some CAD Academy Supers had put in Theodore Roosevelt's nose.

In another clip, a jewelry store heist was in progress. A voice-over explained that using her stellar detective skills, Hawkgirl had been able to ascertain the time and place of the upcoming crime. Security cams caught Hawkgirl flying to the scene, stopping only for a red light, before using her mace to apprehend the culprits. As she turned them over to Police Commissioner Gordon and his officers, Wonder Woman caught a glimpse of his daughter, Barbara Gordon, in the background. At the end of the video, an old woman appeared on the screen.

"¡Hola! Hello, can you hear me?" she said. "Is anyone out there?"

She looks familiar, Wonder Woman thought.

"Soy la abuela de Chica Halcón," the woman said loudly. "I am Hawkgirl's grandmother, her *abuela.*"

Of course! Wonder Woman realized. They had the same nose and no-fuss look about them, softened by their warm brown eyes.

"Hawkgirl, I am so proud of you," Mrs. Muñoz said, her voice breaking. "Your parents would be, too. They had the same sense of justice that you have. To know that their daughter grew up strong and brave, and was awarded this honor . . . well, they would be proud. I love you. *Te amo.*"

Hawkgirl wiped a tear from her eye. So did half the students watching, including Wonder Woman. She hoped that someday she could make her mother that proud.

As The Wall congratulated Hawkgirl, Lois Lane casually

walked over to Wonder Woman. "I may have some information for you," she whispered while pretending to be taking notes on what Waller was saying. "Meet me at the Capes and Cowls Cafe after school."

Wonder Woman always enjoyed going off-campus. There were so many fascinating sights and sounds—like the long line of people waiting outside Bodacious Bob's Beds 'n' Bathtubs for something called a "half-off sale," though Wonder Woman couldn't figure out why anyone would want just half a bathtub.

In Metropolis's Centennial Park, a group of kids were throwing plastic plates back and forth. This seemed to make them happy. As she continued strolling, Wonder Woman saw a little boy sobbing.

"What's the matter?" she asked, rushing over to him.

The boy pointed up. "Save Rainbow!" he begged.

In the tree was a frightened calico kitten. "Of course! What's your name?" Wonder Woman asked as she flew up and gathered the kitty her arms.

"Skipper!" the boy shouted.

"Well, Skipper, here's Rainbow," Wonder Woman said, handing him the cat.

"Thanks, Wonder Woman!" Skipper cried. "I'm never letting go of her!"

With the two friends reunited, Wonder Woman continued toward Main Street, stopping to lift a car for a woman who was changing a tire.

Steve Trevor looked up from Capes & Cowls Cafe's patio, where he was folding napkins. "Hi, Wondy!" he called. "Please take a seat anywhere."

"Oh, okay," Wonder Woman said, picking up a chair and following him inside. She brought it to the counter near him.

"What I meant was . . . ," Steve began. But when she sat next to him, he blushed. "Oh, never mind. That's what I meant."

They grinned at each other.

"I'm meeting Lois Lane," Wonder Woman explained.

"Well, you might be more comfortable over there," Steve said, pointing to an empty booth by the window. "Sometimes it gets crowded after school, so maybe you should snag that one before someone else does."

"Got it!" Wonder Woman said. As she got up, Wonder Woman remembered the kids from the park and how much fun they were having. So she picked up a plate from the counter and threw it at Steve.

The plate hit him on the side of his head, catching him by surprise. "Uh . . . thanks?" he said.

"My pleasure!" Wonder Woman said, smiling brightly.

While Steve went to get ice for his head, Wonder Woman looked out the window. Several passersby waved.

"Does anyone work here?" a teen from another table shouted.

"Be right with you," Steve said. There was an angry welt on his forehead where the plate had hit him. Yet he smiled at Wonder Woman before heading over to a table of three boys wearing CAD Academy letterman's jackets. Their names were embroidered on their backs: Ratcatcher, Captain Cold, and Heat Wave.

Captain Cold was clearly the leader of the group, and the glint in his ice-blue eyes exuded confidence. Something about him looked familiar. Heat Wave acted like he was a big deal, and Ratcatcher, though smaller than the other two, was undeniably sinister.

"I'm so sorry to be late!" Lois exclaimed, rushing over to Wonder Woman. "There are unconfirmed reports that a rocket ship has landed on Earth near a town called Smallville!"

The news shocked Wonder Woman. Suddenly, her problems didn't seem so big.

"I need to go back and file a story about the mystery ship," Lois said. "But first let's talk about you."

"Are you sure?" Wonder Woman asked. "It's no big deal."

"Any time someone is threatened, it's a big deal," Lois said. She took a sip of the smoothie Steve had brought her. "From the way the threats keep arriving just before or after something big happens at your school, I think it's an inside job."

Wonder Woman pondered this. "I think it might be Mandy Bowin," she said.

"It still could be," Lois said. "But maybe she's getting help from someone at Super Hero High. Look at this."

She pushed a familiar piece of paper across the table. It was one of the threatening notes that Wonder Woman had received and sent to Lois. Wonder Woman didn't notice anything odd about the note. It read: *You're getting on my nerves. Go home to Mommy.*

"The note," Lois said. "There's a piece of a logo on the corner. It's from Super Hero High."

Wonder Woman examined the paper.

"I think it might be helpful to have someone who can keep an eye out from inside Super Hero High," Lois Lane said. "Do you know anyone who is able to spy for us?"

Wonder Woman thought long and hard. "I know just the person!" she said. "I'll call her now."

"I was in the area already," Hawkgirl said.

Wonder Woman scooted over so she could sit down.

"Congrats on your award," Lois told her. "You up for an interview later?"

"Okay," Hawkgirl said. "Is that why Wondy asked me to meet you here?"

Lois and Wonder Woman glanced at each other, then filled Hawkgirl in on the whole story. Just as they were finishing, Captain Cold stood up, pounded his chest, and yelled, "CAD

Academy rules! Super Hero High drools!"

"Is that the best you can come up with?" Hawkgirl said, rolling her eyes.

Ratcatcher and Heat Wave laughed as they pulled him back down into his chair.

Wonder Woman blinked at the boys. "Why would they say that?" she asked.

Lois Lane sighed. "Super Hero High is an institution. Many of the most famous super heroes have gone there. CAD Academy is an upstart school. Even though it's only twenty-five years old, it boasts an incredible faculty. Incredible because many of the teachers are reformed super-villains—or at least, they *claim* to be reformed. Super Hero High has its share of the same, but somehow Amanda Waller's vetting system seems more . . . um . . . reliable. Even though CAD Academy advertises that it's for the 'superior super hero,' it's rumored to be a launch pad for bad guys. The real name is Carmine Anderson Dayschool, but most people think CAD stands for Criminals and Delinquents."

Wonder Woman looked sideways at the CAD Academy boys, who were now tossing napkins in the air. As they floated down, Captain Cold froze them with his freeze gun; then Heat Wave blasted them with fire from his flamethrower, and Ratcatcher let out a high-pitched laugh.

"Super Hero High does not consider CAD Academy to be a rival," Lois continued, "but CAD Academy considers Super Hero High theirs."

Steve Trevor was headed toward the CAD Academy table, balancing a full tray of veggie burgers and smoothies. Right before he got there, Wonder Woman saw Ratcatcher take a handful of rat traps out of his pocket and toss them onto the floor.

When Steve set off the traps and started to fall, Wonder Woman flew across the room to catch him, but not before the tray flew up in the air. Before the food and drinks could splatter all over the floor, Hawkgirl was at her side. In a nanosecond, Wonder Woman set Steve down at another table. She and Hawkgirl caught the veggie burgers and two of the smoothies, and the third smoothie landed on Heat Wave.

"I didn't order this," he groused as the pink liquid ran down his face.

"Thanks, little lady," Captain Cold said as he bit into a veggie burger. Wonder Woman glared at him. She wasn't a little lady. In fact, she was bigger and stronger than he was.

"Say, are you two the new waitresses?" Ratcatcher asked as Hawkgirl shoved a handful of rat traps at him. "Because our man Stevie here could sure use some help."

Steve was about to say something, but Lois cut in. "Enjoy your meals boys," she said, leading Wonder Woman and Hawkgirl back to their booth.

"You don't want to mess with those guys," Lois whispered. "They're bad news. Rumor is that some of them are so super rich that whenever they get in trouble at school—which is all the time—their families just bail them out by buying a new building, usually with stolen money."

Wonder Woman heard what Lois was saying. Still, it didn't seem right. She went back to the boys, who were now throwing food at each other.

"Excuse me," she said. "But I think you should apologize to Steve. I know you tried to make him fall on purpose."

Heat Wave stood up. Though he was much taller and wider than Wonder Woman, she didn't flinch.

Steve rushed over. "It's all right, Wondy," he said nervously. "Really!"

By now all the other diners were watching.

Wonder Woman looked at Steve.

"I'm okay," he insisted. Worry flickered in his brown eyes.

She looked back at the CAD Academy boys, who were now snickering, though Wonder Woman couldn't figure out what was so funny.

"I'm okay," they said, mocking Steve.

"Fine," Wonder Woman said, "but if you try to make him fall again, you're going to have to say you're sorry!"

At this, the boys burst into loud laughter.

"Like there's anything you can to do to stop us!" Ratcatcher giggled.

Captain Cold set his gun's sights on Steve, which sent a debilitating chill through him. "Oops," Captain Cold said as his cohorts howled.

Lois and Hawkgirl ran over to Steve, who had dropped to the floor, shivering.

Wonder Woman's eyes narrowed. "I told you to be nice," she said. In a flash she took out her Lasso of Truth and roped all three of them together.

"What is your biggest fear?" she asked, tightening the lasso.

With no choice but to answer truthfully, Heat Wave said, "A spider laying eggs in my ear while I'm sleeping."

Captain Cold said, "Losing."

Ratcatcher said, "Having to give a speech in class."

"Now," Wonder Woman told them, "if you want me to let you go, you have to tell Steve that you're sorry." She paused. "What? I can't hear you."

After the boys glared and grumbled their apologies, Wonder Woman let them go.

"Thanks," Wonder Woman said, and everyone in the diner applauded.

"What just happened?" Ratcatcher asked.

"I dunno," Heat Wave said, "but I don't like the vibe here. Let's go."

As they headed out, Wonder Woman saw that they had written LIVE EVIL with ketchup on the table. "See you at the Super Triathlon—we'll settle our score there!" Captain Cold yelled before the door slammed behind him.

★

Over a week had passed, and Wonder Woman still couldn't get Steve Trevor off her mind.

"He makes me feel funny inside," she told Katana. "And when he thanked me for defending him, I could barely speak. At first I thought he was using his superpowers on me. But I don't think he's a Super. What's happening?"

Katana started laughing.

"What?" Wonder Woman asked, confused.

"Girl," Katana said, "you've got a crush on Steve Trevor!"

Wonder Woman shook her head. That couldn't be possible. *How can Katana be so wrong?* Wonder Woman wondered. She liked Steve too much to ever crush him.

CHAPTER 16

As the weeks rolled past, Wonder Woman felt more at home at Super Hero High. Her once-daily communications to her mother had lagged, and now were often quick replies rather than long messages. She had gotten used to the idiosyncrasies of her fellow Supers—as much as one could. Plus, so many of them were still trying to get their powers under control. Wonder Woman could be having a perfectly normal conversation with someone and suddenly—*whoosh!*—they'd make something catch on fire, or they'd grow an extra arm or two, or they'd vanish and she'd be left standing there looking like she was talking to herself.

One constant was Wonder Woman's roommate, the indomitable Harley Quinn. Like so many other things, Wonder Woman had gotten used to her nonstop videoing, the most recent of which had captured Wonder Woman earning a new school record for the fastest, most efficient Save the Day in school history, right after Superman's. It had been light-years more impressive than her slow-as-molasses save of Mr. Fox from atop the school's Amethyst. Yet with so many classes, and so much homework, plus her clubs, Wonder Woman often found herself stretched thin. Not like Plastic Man, who could stretch his body to impossible lengths. No, Wonder Woman felt stretched thin just from trying to do it all. But she loved it.

Right after lunch one day, Wonder Woman had only a few minutes before Weaponomics class to run to her room and grab her lasso. But before she went in, something stopped her. It was another message. This time, the note was attached to the door with a strange piece of metal. She kept both to show Lois and Hawkgirl.

"Before we begin," Mr. Fox said to his students, "I have a special announcement. He adjusted his red bow tie, which had an L on one side and an F on the other. "As you know, selections are under way for Super Hero High's Super Triathlon team. For those of you who are unaware of how this elite team of teens is chosen, it goes like this." He cleared his throat and put on his glasses before he began to read from the official rulebook.

"'The selection tribunal is made up of three anonymous committees.

"'One. The faculty committee confers and analyzes the students' strengths and abilities.

"'Two. The student committee assesses their leadership and teamwork.

"'Three. The *committee* committee takes the recommendations of the two other committees to make their final recommendations, which are then sent to Principal Waller.'"

Fox lowered the rulebook and added, "While Principal Waller can't add any names to the list, she does have power of veto. Does anyone have any questions?"

Wonder Woman raised her hand.

"Yes, Wonder Woman?" Fox said.

"How many teams compete in the Super Triathlon?"

"According to the rulebook, it starts out with fifty teams, and ends with the top four in the finals. Any other questions? Yes, Wonder Woman?"

"What are the events?"

"Let's see," Fox began. "There are three areas—hence *tri*athalon!

"There's the Interview, which includes a live TV Q-and-A and panel discussion on super hero issues. That's twenty-five percent. Academics counts for twenty-five percent as well, and includes a written test on super hero history, plus a College Bowl–type team competition. But the biggie, weighing in at fifty percent, is the A/P test: Ability/Powers. This includes individual challenges, such as flight, fight, agility, and athleticism."

Many of the Supers, including Wonder Woman, sat up straighter when Mr. Fox talked about this. The A/P test sounded the most exciting.

"Once the final teams are selected," Fox continued, "the scoreboard gets set back to zero and the main competition begins—the super hero obstacle course, which is total A/P all the way. Any other questions? Yes, Wonder Woman?"

"How many students are on each team?"

"There are four members and one alternate. Any other questions? Yes, Wonder Woman?"

"How much time goes into training?"

"Training is seven days a week, twelve hours a day—more as the event nears. Any other questions? Yes, Wonder Woman?"

"How can team members train and go to their classes?"

"Team members are dismissed from most of their classes," Mr. Fox explained. "Students get class credit for their time spent training. Any other questions? Yes . . . Wonder Woman?"

"Do you have a special bow tie for the Super Triathlon?"

Mr. Fox smiled wearily. "Yes," he said. "Are there any other questions?" He looked directly at her. "Anyone besides Wonder Woman?" When she just waved at him, he raised his voice and said, "All right, then! Let's begin with our Weaponomics demonstrations!"

With some startling abilities, and more than a few startling failures, the Supers began demonstrating their skills with weapons. Hawkgirl was up first and confidently approached the test ring. The goal was to disarm the oncoming villains, find the lethal gas canister, and destroy it. With stellar focus, Hawkgirl headed straight for Fox's Fiends, as he called the robot villains—forged in Professor Magnus's very own on-site Metal Man Factory. Without blinking, she maced them with a direct hit, then continued to fly around the burning forest and up to the mountain cave, where the canister, disguised as a stalagmite, was hidden. Scooping it up, she tossed it miles into the air. The canister imploded, and the toxic fumes dissipated before they reached Earth.

As the test was being set up for the next super hero, Hal Jordan came forward. He took a green ring out of his pocket and slipped it on his finger. Wonder Woman had never seen it before. It must be new, she thought.

Instantly, Hal seemed to stand taller and appear stronger. He truly was a Green Lantern. He set his square jaw and took off running at a high speed. Using both his left and right fists—and the rock-solid barrier his ring had formed around his hands—he knocked Fox's Fiends over with a single blow to each. Then Hal began to fly toward the burning forest, but instead of going around or over it, he went right into it, catching himself on fire.

After the safety team doused him with fire-retardant foam, despite his (major) protests, he was benched for the rest of class.

"You look good with foam on your face," Frost said as he

slunk past her. "Like you're ready for a shave."

"Next!" Fox yelled.

Frost strode confidently up to the starting line. Acting as if she did this all the time, she spun around and froze Fox's Fiends around her. Then she ran toward the mountain that was ablaze with fire. Standing her ground, Frost absorbed the heat from the flames so that not even an ember remained. She raced up to the cave and froze the canister, causing the lethal gas to crystallize into tiny pellets, none of which were lethal on their own. Then she tossed the pellets into the wind, scattering them in a million different directions.

Katana was next. She cartwheeled up to the starting line armed with three weapons: a samurai sword, a katana blade, and a *sai*—a pointy pronged baton like the one fellow student Lady Shiva wielded. Katana studied all three before tossing the *sai* aside. Then, with amazing precision, she fought the Fox Fiends with her samurai sword, defeating them all before heading to the burning forest. There, she took out her namesake katana blade and cut down the burning trees with such speed that the fires were extinguished. Taking hold of one of the smoldering logs, Katana catapulted herself up into the mountain cave. With super-speed, she attached the hilt of her sword to the hook on the canister and whirled it over her head. Like a shot put, she heaved it into the air, where it landed in Poison Lake and was consumed by the other toxins.

"Wonder Woman," Mr. Fox called out. "You're up!"

"No, I'm right here," she answered, tapping him on the shoulder.

Mr. Fox adjusted his bow tie. "Over there, Wonder Woman," he said, pointing to the starting line. "You may begin whenever you are ready."

Wonder Woman took a deep breath. She thought about what Lucius Fox had said about the teacher committee and wondered if he was on it. Either way, she wanted to make a good impression.

She decided to approach Fox's Fiends from the air, where she'd have a tactical advantage. However, even through the Fiends were audio-animatronics, they were capable of guessing their opponent's moves. They were clearly some of Professor Magnus's greatest inventions to date. Soon they were in the air, too, and that was their mistake. Wonder Woman got out her lasso and was about to rope them when one sent out dual laser beams.

"Okay, you asked for it!" Wonder Woman said, raising both bracelets in the air. The lasers bounced off them and back to Fox's Fiends, causing them to short-circuit.

Wonder Woman flew over the burning forest, then circled it, getting closer and closer to the fire with each lap. She sped up, agitating the air and creating pressure waves that displaced the oxygen and put out the flames. With the fire out, she was free to address the lethal gas. Throwing it as hard as she could into outer space, Wonder Woman tossed her tiara and it collided with the canister, detonating it and creating a fireworks display before returning back to her.

"Well done, Wonder Woman," Mr. Fox said appreciatively. "Well done!"

Cheetah, who was watching from the sidelines, growled.

★

During phys ed, Wonder Woman was still in a happy mood. As the class ran a twenty-mile warm-up, Hawkgirl caught up with her.

"I've got some news you're going to want to hear, and some news you're not going to want to hear," Hawkgirl said.

As the two ran side by side, Hawkgirl continued, "Bumblebee hears things. Sometimes on purpose. Sometimes by accident. Either way, she has the buzz, so I asked her if she was working in Waller's office the day Mandy Bowin was expelled."

"Was she?" Wonder Woman asked.

Hawkgirl nodded. "Bumblebee heard Mandy begging, 'Please, please, Principal Waller!' and The Wall saying, 'No, I will not allow it!'"

"So maybe Cheetah was right. She was forced out," Wonder Woman mused. "I wonder how that feels. It must be awful. And it's all my fault."

"It is not," said Hawkgirl. "The Wall never does anything on a whim. She must have had her reasons. Besides, we don't have concrete evidence of this. Here's the news I didn't think you'd want to hear. Remember that note and blade you gave me?"

Wonder Woman nodded. Both girls were quiet as Golden Glider sped past them, followed by Star Sapphire, with Miss Martian trailing behind her.

Hawkgirl continued. "That blade had to come from somewhere. Remember when Katana threw her *sai* aside in Weaponomics? Well, that's because one tip of the forked blade was missing. However, it's not missing at all. It's right here." Hawkgirl held up the broken blade from Wonder Woman's door. "It's a perfect match," she said.

CHAPTER 17

Before she confronted Katana, Wonder Woman wanted to talk to Lois and Hawkgirl together. Earlier that day, someone had sealed her locker shut by melting the metal. And even though Wonder Woman had handed in her history assignment early, Liberty Belle said it was missing and gave her a zero.

"Where are you off to?" Katana asked as Wonder Woman shut her dorm room door.

Wonder Woman froze. "Just somewhere in Metropolis," she said, sounding vague.

"I'll go with you!" Katana volunteered.

Before Wonder Woman could say anything, Katana had invited Bumblebee.

"Can I go?" Harley asked as she linked arms with them.

Poison Ivy joined them in the dorm hallway. "Is this a party?" she asked. "Are you having a party? It's okay if I wasn't invited."

"Come with us," Katana said. "We're all going to Metropolis!"

Hawkgirl came out of her room. "Are you ready?" She looked surprised to see everyone surrounding Wonder Woman.

Wonder Woman shrugged. "We've got company," she said.

As they weaved their way through the bustling streets of Metropolis, stopping to sign autographs and save lives, Hawkgirl hung back with Katana. Wonder Woman tried to overhear what they were saying, but it was difficult with Harley talking nonstop.

"So, my numbers are definitely up," Harley boasted. "HQTV is getting so many hits that I could even get a sponsor if I wanted to. I've decided to stay independent; that way I have total control over the content. But Star Sapphire said her parents may be interested in buying part of HQTV, and—"

Wonder Woman wished she had super-hearing, like some of the others. At one point, Wonder Woman could see Katana's angry face leaning in toward Hawkgirl, and Hawkgirl standing firm. What were they saying to each other?

In Centennial Park, Wonder Woman saw a familiar sight.

"Wonder Woman!" Skipper cried. "Rainbow is stuck in the tree again!"

Sure enough, the calico kitten was perched on an upper

branch. Only this time, instead of looking scared, Rainbow looked proud of herself. As Wonder Woman and Bumblebee flew up to retrieve the kitten, Poison Ivy examined a bed of brown, dead roses, and Harley videotaped the rescue.

With Rainbow safely in Skipper's arms, Harley put down her camera. "Hey, would you two mind doing that again?" she asked. "Bumblebee, toss the kitten to Wonder Woman. That'll make for a much better video!"

Wonder Woman wrinkled her brow. "But that wouldn't be real," she said.

Bumblebee nodded. "If you want real, maybe we can re-rescue Rainbow!"

Harley laughed. "Real isn't as important as a compelling visual," she explained to them.

"She's right," someone said. "Image is everything. Trust me."

They turned around to see Golden Glider skating past them and sipping a purple acai smoothie in a Capes & Cowls Cafe to-go cup. "Have fun, ladies!" She held up her hand and waved to the group. "Be good!"

Wonder Woman noticed Poison Ivy smiling as if she had a secret. "What is it?" she asked her.

"Not much, not yet," Poison Ivy said, glancing back as they continued toward the Capes & Cowls Cafe. Where once was a patch of brown, Wonder Woman could see a bed of blooming red roses.

Steve Trevor turned the same shade of red as the ketchup bottle he was holding when he saw Wonder Woman. She did the same. Both tried to pretend they couldn't hear Katana laughing.

As the girls were sitting down, Lois Lane arrived. "Wow, uh, Wondy and Hawkgirl, what a surprise bumping into you two here," she said.

"But we had planned—" Wonder Woman started to say.

Before she could finish, Hawkgirl jumped in. "Yes, it's a *surprise* to see you here, too!" she said to Lois.

Ah! Okay. Wonder Woman nodded. She got it! She had almost forgotten that she had called a *secret* meeting with her sleuthing friends.

"What a total SURPRISE seeing you here, Lois Lane," Wonder Woman said. "So UNEXPECTED. Won't you join us?"

Wonder Woman winked at Hawkgirl, who ignored her. So she winked again and again until Hawkgirl kicked her under the table.

"Sure, why not," Lois said casually. "I'd love to join you."

"Well, well, look who's leaving," Hawkgirl said pointing to the back table.

Ratcatcher, Captain Cold, and Heat Wave from CAD Academy were sneaking out the back door.

"Hi, guys!" Wonder Woman said, waving. "No hard feelings, I hope!"

"No hard feelings," Captain Cold said, shoving the tray of food Steve was carrying into his chest.

"Hey!" Wonder Woman protested. "I thought you were going to start being nice to Steve."

She reached for her lasso, but Steve stopped her. "Wonder Woman, it's okay. Really," he said as the remains of a spinach salad ran down his shirt. "Please don't do that."

"Okay," she said, returning to her seat.

She could hear the boys outside chanting, "Live evil!"

For the rest of the time at the diner, it seemed that Steve was trying to avoid Wonder Woman. When he brought her favorite kale chips and strawberry banana smoothie, he didn't look her in the eye. Wonder Woman wondered if she had done something wrong.

The girls chatted and chewed and had a great time discussing the upcoming Super Triathlon. Everyone had guesses about who'd be on the team. Wonder Woman tried not to get excited when her name kept coming up. At last, when all the smoothies were drained and all the kale chips and veggie pizzas had been devoured, it was time to go.

"You all go ahead," Hawkgirl said to the others. "Wondy and I have some errands to run in town."

"We do?" Wonder Woman asked, surprised. She couldn't remember what that might be. When she saw Hawkgirl giving her a hard look, she got it. "We do, we do," she said.

"Errands, lots of them. Yep. Errands. To run. We're going to run to do the errands!"

Harley, Katana, and Poison Ivy took off, and Lois, Hawkgirl, and Wonder Woman stayed back.

"I thought they'd never leave!" Hawkgirl exclaimed. "If I have to hear another Harley Quinn knock-knock joke, I think I'll explode."

"So," Lois said, looking at Wonder Woman, "what do you have for me?"

"I still think it's Mandy," she said. "But now my grades are being compromised!"

Hawkgirl took out the tip of the blade. "It's not Katana," she said, pushing it across the table. "Katana said she was surprised to find the prong of her *sai* missing during the Weaponomics demonstration."

"Do you believe her?" Lois asked.

"I do," Hawkgirl said. "And her roommate, Poison Ivy, says the she didn't leave her room that morning until after Wondy found the threatening note on her door."

Lois wrote something down. "Okay, but that doesn't necessarily clear her. Katana is really stealthy. She could have slipped away without Poison Ivy noticing. Ivy tends to get caught up in her own world."

"But why would Katana want me out?" Wonder Woman asked. It made no sense.

"That's true," Hawkgirl added. "Katana has been a real friend to Wondy. However . . ."

As Hawkgirl filled Lois in on what Bumblebee had overheard between Principal Waller and Mandy Bowin, Wonder Woman watched Steve. He had returned to filling up the ketchup bottles and had lined them all up on the counter. She was impressed by the straight row he had made.

"Well, I have some information for the two of you," Lois said, referring to her green reporter's notebook. "Mandy has enrolled in an elite music conservatory. From what I could dig up, she seems happy and has not told anyone that she used to go to Super Hero High.

"So I took the liberty of asking Barbara Gordon to do some online sleuthing, and she found out that on Mandy's Our Space page, she had written: *Mandy Bowin, out. Wonder Woman, in. Someone's super happy.* But she deleted it almost as soon as she had written it.

So there it was. The evidence that Mandy was bitter. She must have been embarrassed to have been expelled. But what had she done that was so bad? Or had Principal Waller really dumped her, like Cheetah and some of the other kids were saying, to let Wonder Woman in? If that was the case, Wonder Woman felt she owed Mandy an apology. If it was Mandy trying to bring her down, Wonder Woman wanted to meet her and find out why.

Wonder Woman was getting dizzy with all the Mandy Bowin possibilities. *How can someone I don't even know have this power over me?* she thought.

CHAPTER 18

The next week was worse. Much worse.

Every morning, Wonder Woman awoke to a mailbox filled with cryptic messages.

Beware, Wonder Woman, your time is running out.

Your powers are nothing compared to mine. Want to see?

Don't bother saving the world—save yourself instead!

Other than Hawkgirl, Wonder Woman wasn't sure whom she could trust, and she wanted to trust everyone. However, Katana did have a missing blade. At the last Science Club meeting, Poison Ivy accidentally blew up the Powerful Power Powder that Wonder Woman was concocting. And Harley was always posting embarrassing videos of her.

"There are some super heroes among us who will go on to be great leaders and role models," Principal Waller was saying at the assembly. "There are others who will tap into the dark side, and—though our goal is to help you avoid this—

go on to be super-villains." There was a discernible shift in the audience as the Supers glanced suspiciously at some of their classmates.

"Our next Super Hero of the Month is in the first category," The Wall continued.

Wonder Woman held her breath. She had crossed so many things off of her to-do list, but not this one. Not yet. Other than her life being threatened, and being made fun of on HQTV, and her mother telling her she might be pulled out of school, and her weird feelings of pleasing discomfort when she saw Steve Trevor, things had been going really well for Wonder Woman. Maybe this would be her month!

"Our next Super Hero of the Month is . . ."

Wonder Woman sat up straight and adjusted her tiara. The more she thought about it, the more it made sense that it might be her. She had been doing well in her classes, had saved several lives, and had earned honors, like her school record for Save the Day.

When Principal Waller announced the next ambassador, Wonder Woman stood up!

"Poison Ivy, please come up to the stage," Waller said.

Surprised, Wonder Woman quickly sat down as the rest of the students leapt up to cheer Poison Ivy on.

"You really didn't think you'd win, did you?" Cheetah asked, laughing.

"I . . . I . . . ," Wonder Woman stammered.

"I know," Frost jumped in. "I know you're full of yourself."

Wonder Woman shivered as she watched her friend make her way to the stage. Poison Ivy glowed with such happiness that when she laughed, flowers rained down from the auditorium's ceiling.

"This student," Principal Waller exclaimed, plucking a daffodil from her shoulder and tossing it aside, "has done something extraordinary for the city of Metropolis, and in turn for all of us."

As the video began to play, the students were treated to a desolate display of dirt and rocks. *THEN* appeared on the screen. In the next scene, the same area had been transformed, and *NOW* appeared over a bountiful garden of fruits and vegetables.

"Thanks to Poison Ivy and her love of plants and science, this community garden benefits all of our Metropolis neighbors. Created to help the hungry, there is enough food here to feed dozens of individuals and families."

To Wonder Woman's surprise, Steve Trevor appeared on the screen. He looked nervous.

"Um, hey," he said. "Are you recording? Oh, you are? Okay. My name's Steve, and I'm a volunteer here at Met Fam Farm. Er, that's what we call Metropolis Family Farm. Thanks to Poison Ivy, those in need have a place to get wholesome fresh food. Um, is the video camera still on? Can I do this over?"

Poison Ivy was totally deserving of the title, Wonder Woman reminded herself. Totally, completely, awesomely deserving. Even if Ivy hadn't meant to create a community farm, but had instead been trying to build something entirely different . . . a new weapon made of plants that did your bidding.

Dr. Arkham released an audible sigh when Wonder Woman wanted to talk rather than take her weekly power nap. He put his pillow back under his desk and sat up straight in his chair.

"Yes, yes, well, stress is something that even the most adept super heroes have to learn to cope with," Dr. Arkham said as he pressed his fingertips together. "I do hope all the books I've been giving you have helped."

Wonder Woman didn't tell him that she had resorted to speed-reading. Unfortunately, whether she read them fast or slow, Wonder Woman still didn't understand what they were about.

"A young super hero's life can be divided into four categories," Dr. Arkham said. "School, social life, sports, sleep," he continued. "Pick three."

"But I want to do all four," Wonder Woman insisted.

"Tsk, tsk," Arkham said. "Impossible! Which one are you going to do without?"

"Sleep?" Wonder Woman said. She thought they had already established that.

"Are you sure?" Dr. Arkham asked.

"Social?" Wonder Woman said.

"Are you sure?" Dr. Arkham asked.

"Sports?" Wonder Woman said.

"Are you sure?" Dr. Arkham asked.

"School?" Wonder Woman said.

"Are you sure?" Dr. Arkham asked.

This went on for the rest of the hour, leaving Wonder Woman thoroughly confused and unsure of what she really wanted. As they shook hands at the end of the session, Dr. Arkham yawned. "Goodbye, Wonder Woman. See you next week. And in the meantime, remember, no stress!"

All the Supers were on their best behavior. The Super Triathlon team was to be announced soon, and no one knew who the selection committee members were, which meant that they had to impress everyone. It was exhausting, especially for the students who had trouble being nice.

"Your hair doesn't look half bad today," Star Sapphire said to Wonder Woman. Golden Glider looked up from polishing her skates and laughed.

"Your speech on 'Super Heroes Who Lived On Islands' wasn't totally boring," Frost told Wonder Woman.

"I don't like you," Cheetah said.

Okay, maybe not all the super heroes were being nice to each other. And someone was being especially not nice to

Wonder Woman. The stakes were getting higher. The latest threat had come in the form of a present. Wonder Woman had eagerly opened the pink box tied with a purple ribbon, but when she took off the lid, an army of mice exploded into the room.

"Cripes!" Harley had cried as the mice rained down on them. "If you're going to do that, at least warn me so I can video it!"

"What is going on?" The Wall demanded. A thick file labeled *W. Woman* flew over to her. Without taking her eyes off Wonder Woman, Principal Waller snatched the file out of the air. "Thank you, Bumblebee," she said.

Wonder Woman watched her friend buzz away and then turn big again before closing the office door behind her.

"Going on?" Wonder Woman repeated. "Um, I heard my hair only looks half bad today?"

There was silence as Principal Waller reviewed the file. Wonder Woman could see that it was from Dr. Arkham. When she finally put the folder down, The Wall asked, "Wonder Woman, what can you tell me about the mouse explosion in your dorm room?"

"Oh, that!" Wonder Woman said, wondering if she was in trouble. "All the mice survived."

"Wonder Woman," Principal Waller cautioned, "explosions outside the classroom are forbidden." Wonder Woman saw that the principal was frowning, so she frowned, too. "I need you to tell me who did it," Principal Waller continued. "Was it you or Harley? Or someone else?"

"I can't tell you," Wonder Woman said. She didn't know the answer, and that was the truth.

"I see," said Waller. "Harley claims it began raining mice, but she doesn't know why or how. So I was hoping your memory was intact."

"My memory still works," Wonder Woman said. She closed her eyes and thought about her mother.

As if reading her mind, Principal Waller said, "Your mother wanted me to look out for you. I'm trying to do that, Wonder Woman." She picked up the file. "Dr. Arkham seems to think that you're very stressed. Is that true?"

Wonder Woman thought about it. Yes, she was stressed. But so was every student at Super Hero High. The training was grueling. Expectations were high. So much was demanded of them. Lives depended on it.

"I may be a little stressed," Wonder Woman admitted.

"Hmm," Principal Waller said, referring to a sheet of paper. "Seventeen clubs is a lot to be in. I'd recommend you pick one or two and drop the rest. As for the mouse explosion, if you're covering for Harley, you're not helping her."

"It's my fault!" Wonder Woman blurted. She didn't want

to get her roommate in trouble for something she didn't do. If only she could figure out who was causing the commotions, then she could put a stop to it.

"I see," the principal said. " I'm afraid I'm going to have to send you to after-school detention. You know the detention rules, don't you? *Check your weapons, power down, and pay your dues!* At the end of the week, if no other rules have been broken, you can resume your normal life."

What is normal? Wonder Woman asked herself.

"Do you have any questions?"

This was her chance. Should she ask? Principal Waller wouldn't have asked if she had questions if she wasn't willing to answer them, right?

"I do have one question," Wonder Woman said. She was relieved that she'd finally get her answer.

"What is it?" Principal Waller said as she walked her to the door.

Wonder Woman gulped and blurted, "Is it true that you expelled Mandy Bowin to make room for me at Super Hero High?"

PART THREE

CHAPTER 19

Wonder Woman was impressed. She had no idea someone could glare for so long without blinking. Finally, The Wall crossed her strong arms, arched an eyebrow, and said in her *how-dare-you* voice, "You weren't talking to *me*, were you?"

Wonder Woman was speechless. She thought she'd been talking to her, but now she wasn't so sure. Never in her time at Super Hero High had Wonder Woman felt so scared. Not when the Scarecrow was testing his new Fear Gas in Science Club and Wonder Woman couldn't stop cringing for two days. Not when she'd walked into a history midterm test that she didn't know about. Not when she ate goat cheese for the first time.

"Student. Files. Are. NEVER. Discussed," Principal Waller stated firmly. "Not Mandy's, not yours, no one's! Instead of worrying about someone who is not here, you ought to worry about yourself!"

"But . . . ," Wonder Woman started to say. She shook her

head and slowly backed out of the room. "I'm sorry," she mouthed. "So sorry."

And she was. She was sorry that she had brought up the question, and she was sorry that it was even a question in the first place. Wonder Woman had ignited the wrath of The Wall. Had Principal Waller insinuated that she would be the next person expelled? Then what? Back to Paradise Island as a failure? What would her mother think?

As Wonder Woman wandered down the hallway, Bumblebee sped up to her and gave her a hug. No words were needed.

By the time she got to phys ed, class was halfway over. Even though the relay race was something Wonder Woman normally excelled in, today she could hardly focus.

"Next two teams!" Wildcat growled as he looked at his students. His grisly voice and stocky build belied his speed and agility. Everyone shifted nervously. Wildcat was known to pounce with deadly accuracy when confronted.

Team One was made up of Hawkgirl and Green Lantern, with Cheetah anchoring. Team Two featured Star Sapphire, Beast Boy, and Wonder Woman bringing up the rear. The fifty-mile course circled Super Hero High three times and then wound through the forest, along the cliffs, and down by the river and ended up back where the race had started. Instead of passing a baton, each team passed a fully charged Shock Stick.

"An added incentive to run fast," Wildcat explained. There

was a mischievous twinkle in his eyes. "The Shock Sticks are specially calibrated. If you slow down, you will be zapped. If you stop, you will be zapped. If you complain, you will be zapped. However, if and when you make it to the finish line within the allotted amount of time, just toss your stick into the defusing bin, where it will harmlessly deactivate. Any questions? No? Good. Go!"

The first two legs of each team did well, as expected. When the sticks were handed to the last runners, the air crackled with bolts of blue electricity. Cheetah and Wonder Woman started off running stride for stride, neither one letting up, neither one out of breath. As they neared the forest, Cheetah asked, "How's your life, Wonder Woman?"

When Wonder Woman started to answer, Cheetah just laughed. *Is everything all right?* Wonder Woman asked herself. She was so busy thinking about the anonymous messages that when they turned a sharp corner along the cliffs, Wonder Woman accidentally bumped into her opponent.

As Cheetah tumbled down the rocky mountain, her roar could be heard all the way back in the teacher's lounge.

Instantly, Wonder Woman flew to where Cheetah had landed on the rocks.

"My leg! My leg! Ouch!" Cheetah cried out. "I'm hurt."

Wonder Woman reached toward Cheetah, but she batted her away. "You've done enough damage already, don't you think?"

Wonder Woman's eyes teared up. "I am so sorry," she said.

"Go get Wildcat," Cheetah growled. "I don't need any more help from you!"

Suddenly, there was a huge electric burst that could be seen over the tops of the trees.

The Shock Sticks had gone off, and the resulting mega-shock wave caused some of the nearby rocks to fall. Wonder Woman grabbed Cheetah and flew to safety as the two watched the rest of the rocks tumble down. Had Wonder Woman not reacted so quickly, they both would have been crushed.

Wonder Woman was speechless, but Cheetah was not. "This was all your fault. Don't think I'm going to forget this, Wonder Woman."

★

That Cheetah clearly despised Wonder Woman wore on her. Couldn't Cheetah see it had been an accident? She would never have hurt her on purpose.

Cheetah was hobbling around on crutches, her leg bandaged, telling anyone who would listen that it was Wonder Woman's fault. Harley scored an exclusive interview with Cheetah. Cheetah told her, "I don't know if I'll ever walk again, thanks to Wonder Woman. Ouch! Ouch! Oh, ouch! I'm in such pain! Ouch."

Though few took Cheetah's constant complaints and

accusations seriously, it didn't stop them from passing along the gossip. After the accident, the online chatter ramped up tenfold. Everyone had an opinion about Wonder Woman, and for the first time, she was cast as a villain.

Poor Cheetah, one person wrote. *She was a frontrunner for Super Hero High's Super Triathlon team. Could it be that Wonder Woman pushed her off a cliff to make sure Cheetah wouldn't make the team?*

Rumors of a rivalry between Cheetah and Wonder Woman ran rampant. Wonder Woman tried to shake them off, and was actually glad she had after-school detention because no one was allowed to talk there. Plus it gave her time to finalize her design for Crazy Quilt's class. The big costume presentation was coming up, and it helped take her mind off the gossip, which hurt more than the crush of rocks would have.

When at last the time came for Wonder Woman's costume unveiling, the room was abuzz. Literally. Bumblebee's costume had malfunctioned again, sending electrical stings all around the classroom, which heightened the excitement. This was a big deal. If done right, a super hero costume could become iconic. If done wrong, they could be featured on Harley's new video segment *Fashion, Function, or Failure?*

Crazy Quilt had erected a catwalk down the middle of his loftlike classroom. Supers sat along the sides in folding chairs. Crazy Quilt himself occupied what looked like a lifeguard chair, cradling his clipboard as he critiqued each outfit.

"Wonder Woman! Let's see what you've got!" Crazy Quilt called through a megaphone, even though a megaphone wasn't necessary in the small room.

"Don't mess up," Golden Glider said to Wonder Woman with a playful grin, blowing snowflakes at her.

"Good luck, partner," Star Sapphire whispered. "Do well for us!"

"Thank you!" Wonder Woman said brightly. Without Star Sapphire, her costume wouldn't be half as good it was. Though it was Katana who'd helped Wonder Woman the most, it was Star Sapphire who'd insisted that Wonder Woman keep the long cape.

"Your stumble was purely from inexperience," Star Sapphire said kindly. "Nothing beats the majestic flow of a regal Amazonian cape in action." Her violet ring glowed as Golden Glider nodded in agreement.

The crowd gasped when Wonder Woman stepped onto the stage. Her costume looked fresh, but familiar at the same time. Simple . . . yet functional . . . smart . . . yet stylish. Katana had guided Wonder Woman, who had used organic materials recommended by Poison Ivy. The color palette was bold, as suggested by Harley, and the red, blue, and gold complemented each other. Hawkgirl had suggested a clasp on her belt to secure the Lasso of Truth when it was not in use.

Wonder Woman's pants were bright royal blue with white stars lining the outside seams and a stylish belt of gold around the waist. Her bright red shirt, with capped sleeves, was topped with a golden collar that featured stacked double *W*s flaring out like wings on her shoulders. High but flat red boots accented with gold piping and white wings completed her look. And much to Katana's obvious dismay, Wonder Woman did choose to wear the cape that Star Sapphire had suggested. There was no denying that it brought an air of ceremony as well as spectacle to the princess's costume, but Wonder Woman liked the addition.

Crazy Quilt pressed the button on a vintage boom box, and disco music began to play as Wonder Woman stepped up her stride. Her friends cheered. Suddenly, a trio of barrels was shot at her. She raised her bracelets and deflected them. As the barrels bounced off the walls, the ceiling opened and a vat of orange Jell-O tilted, poised to splash its contents on Wonder Woman. She leapt out of the way, nearly tripping on one of the barrels. It wasn't just a catwalk—it was an obstacle course!

"We want to test fashion and function," Crazy Quilt said from his lifeguard chair. His eyes sparkled with glee. "Keep going, Wonder Woman. Let's see what you and your costume are made of!"

Thrilled, Wonder Woman continued down the runway, batting away rubber bullets with her bracelets, lassoing oncoming drones, jumping over hungry reptiles. Suddenly, the Save the Day alarm went off. This time, Wonder Woman didn't hesitate. She called to Bumblebee, Hawkgirl, and Katana. "Let's go!"

The foursome rushed to the top of the administrative building, where the alert was coming from, and stopped cold. Looking up, they saw an incredible scene. A trio of teachers wearing matching sweatshirts had captured Principal Waller and locked her—and her desk—in a sealed glass jail that was perched precariously on the ledge of the roof. If not for the tiny air holes, The Wall would not have been able to breathe for long.

"What does the 'EV' on their sweatshirts mean?" Wonder Woman asked Hawkgirl as they flew over to get a better view. Wonder Woman's long cape was giving her an aerodynamic edge, and she could feel the extra surge of power.

"Evil Villain," Hawkgirl explained. "Teachers wear EV sweatshirts during the drills when they're playing bad guys. Although Waller always reminds us that real villains aren't always that easy to spot."

"I'm getting bored in here, Supers," Principal Waller bellowed as she shuffled paperwork at her desk. She looked at her watch. "Someone better get me out of here fast, or everyone is in trouble!"

The glass jail seemed to be magically getting smaller and smaller—or else Principal Waller was getting bigger. Soon she would be squished!

Katana was scaling the building. Lagging behind her was Cheetah with her injured leg.

"Why don't you just take the elevator," Green Lantern asked as he flew past them.

The flyers hovered, looking for a way to break Principal Waller out. A few Supers, like Miss Martian, stayed on the ground, not knowing what to do. In the distance, a gray mass had enveloped the clouds and was threatening to storm over Super Hero High.

Harley caught it all on video.

Cheetah and Katana were close to the top of the building.

"I can get Waller out," Poison Ivy said from below. Only Wonder Woman heard her. She flew back down.

"How?" she asked.

"This," Poison Ivy said, holding out her hand. A small seed rested in her palm. "I just need to get it into the box."

Wonder Woman shouted, "Bumblebee, I have a job for you!"

"What's up?" Bumblebee asked.

"Fly with me and I'll fill you in," Wonder Woman said. "Thanks, Ivy!"

Bumblebee made herself small and entered the glass jail through one of the air holes.

"Oh, hello," Principal Waller said, looking nonplussed. The glass ceiling was practically touching the top of her head.

By then Katana and Cheetah had made it to the roof and were arguing over what to do. Katana was trying to break the glass, and Cheetah was looking for a hidden door.

"Bumblebee, do your thing!" Wonder Woman yelled. She flew higher to get a better view. A gust of wind swirled the cape around and suddenly Wonder Woman was flying *backward.* As she tried to adjust, Wonder Woman got more tangled up in the material. Instead of rescuing Principal Waller, Wonder Woman worried that someone might have to rescue *her.* She began to plummet. . . .

CHAPTER 20

The ground came rushing up so fast, Wonder Woman had less than a nanosecond to react. The clasp around her neck that attached the cape to her costume was jammed! In one yank, she ripped it off, and she screeched to a halt inches before she would have slammed into the hard concrete walkway.

As the cape landed on top of Star Sapphire, the other students cheered Wonder Woman's close call. However, this did not help The Wall. She was still stuck in her glass jail, only now she had company. Bumblebee grew to her full size and smiled at Waller. But her smile was met with a glare.

"Excuse me," Principal Waller called down wearily. "But this is no time to play with your cape! Will someone please save the day?"

Wonder Woman rose into the air, higher and faster now without the weight of the unwieldy cape. "Do it now,

Bumblebee," she said, pushing the seed through an air hole to her friend. "Get Principal Waller in the corner with you, throw the seed, stand back, and I'll handle the rest!"

Everyone applauded when Bumblebee hurled the seed against the ground, and it immediately grew into a tree so big and strong that it broke through the glass, shattering it. As Waller began to fall, Wonder Woman scooped her up. Several of the other flyers were able to grab her desk and collect her papers as they rained over the school.

If the Supers thought it was over, they were wrong. The gray mass swelled, and lightning began to shoot out of the storm clouds. Wonder Woman looked around. Hawkgirl and Beast Boy—who was in bat form—were flying back to school, just ahead of the mass. Supers began to scatter.

"I got this," someone said.

Wonder Woman turned to see Golden Glider digging her skates into the icy ground that had materialized around her. With all her might, she conjured up her powers and sent a blast of subzero arctic air into the center of the gray cloud, which looked to be several city blocks wide. Almost instantly, it began to freeze and fall. But before it could cause damage, Katana stepped up and threw her sword, shattering the ice so hard, it turned into hail!

The hail had melted and was just a memory by the time everyone filed into the auditorium.

"A special thank-you to Professor Ivo's Cybernetic

Wildstorm Cloud, the icing on today's Save the Day drill,"
Principal Waller said as Golden Glider and Katana high-
fived. "And more importantly," she continued, "well done,
Supers, for your teamwork. Well done!"

When the Supers returned to their classes, Crazy Quilt
looked up from the fashion magazine he was perusing. It was
dated September 1976.

"Ah, you're all back at last," he declared. "Wonder Woman,
I have never seen anything like that!"

"The Save the Day rescue?" she asked.

"No, no, no," he said, motioning to a computer where
Harley's video had been live streaming. "I've never seen
someone design a costume in midair. It was a bold move!
When you tossed aside that hideous cape, it was an inspired
moment of fashion meeting function. Clap, clap!" he called
out. "Everyone, let's clap for Wonder Woman and her A-plus-
plus in costume design!"

Not everyone clapped.

When Wonder Woman got back to her dorm room, Harley
was logging the number of views on her Save the Day video.

"We've got a huge following," she exclaimed. "The WWWs are in full force right now!"

Wonder Woman wasn't looking at the computer. Instead, she focused on the cream-colored envelope on her pillow. Inside was another note. This time it read *Beware and be gone. This is not a joke, even if you are.*

"Where are you going?" Harley asked as Wonder Woman headed out the door.

"To see some friends," she said.

The weekly Metropolis Farmers Market had taken over most of Centennial Park. Colorful tents were crammed with tables heavy with fresh fruits and vegetables, breads and brownies, sacks of grains, and bags of nuts. Poison Ivy looked lonesome sitting at a table with a handmade sign that read *Super Delicious Poison Apples!* Sadly, no one was buying them.

Wonder Woman purchased three apples—she knew that they were only named after Poison Ivy, not really poisonous—and headed to the Buttery Bakery Homemade Pie booth.

"I'd like one," she said, pointing at a cherry pie with a golden brown lattice crust.

"One slice of pie coming up!" the woman said. Her cheeks were as ruddy as the cherries.

"No, the whole pie, please," Wonder Woman said. "And no need to wrap it up. I'll eat it now."

"That's my girl," the woman said, smiling.

Wonder Woman smiled back and didn't correct her. She wasn't that lady's girl. Her mom lived on Paradise Island. Wonder Woman took a photo of the pie for her mother.

Captain Cold and his cronies from CAD Academy walked past, making piggy noises.

"What?" Wonder Woman asked. The pie was starting to disappear fast. "I don't get it."

"You're eating a whole pie," Heat Wave pointed out.

"Yes!" Wonder Woman agreed. "And it's delish!"

When Wonder Woman spotted Lois and Hawkgirl weaving through the crowd, she ran up and handed over the latest note. Lois read it first, then handed her Mandy's address.

"You don't stand a chance," Captain Cold said as the boys took their time strolling past.

"Excuse me?" Wonder Woman answered. Did he know something about Mandy?

"The Super Triathlon. Super Hero High does not stand a chance," he repeated. "Everyone knows that CAD Academy will come home with the title, just like we did the last time."

"Yeah! We got a guaranteed win!" Ratcatcher bragged before Captain Cold shut him down with a frosty look.

"Live evil!" the CAD Academy boys kept chanting as they retreated. "Live evil!" Even after they were gone, everyone could hear them.

"So glad they're out of here," Lois said. "Wondy, that's the address you asked for. What are you going to do with it?"

"I'm going to go see Mandy," she said. "And apologize."

"For what?" Hawkgirl asked. "You didn't do anything wrong. For all we know, this Mandy person could be dangerous!"

"If she is, I want to find out," Wonder Woman said. "And if she isn't, well, I want to find out why she left Super Hero High."

"I'm not so sure you should just show up at her house . . . ," Lois said, thinking out loud.

"But if Mandy knows she's coming, and she's the guilty party, it could be dangerous for Wondy," Hawkgirl reasoned.

"What are you going to do?" Lois asked.

"I'll know when I get there," Wonder Woman said. She returned to the Buttery Bakery booth. "May I have another pie?" she asked.

"Sure thing!" the lady said. "You want this one for here or to go?"

"To go, please," Wonder Woman said, explaining, "There's someplace I need to be."

CHAPTER 21

From the clouds, Wonder Woman watched her friends and fellow students milling about, munching on roasted corn on the cob and causing general mischief and mayhem. She could not believe how far removed Metropolis was from Paradise Island's tropical seas, gently swaying palm trees, and Greek palaces. Still, Wonder Woman loved both places fiercely and could not imagine being without either one. The mere thought of ever having to leave Super Hero High weighed heavily on her.

Later, as Wonder Woman consulted a map and flew toward a remote area of Metropolis called Hobb's Bay, she saw a huge suspension bridge stretched across a calm blue sea. Curious seagulls flew alongside her before veering off to places unknown. Wonder Woman continued over a steep, crooked road and then hovered over a purple Victorian house with pink trim and gingerbread details on the eaves. There was a yellow bicycle with a flowered basket on the porch.

Music wafted from one of the open upstairs windows.

Wonder Woman had never heard anything so beautiful in her life. It was as if the music were calling out to her, pulling her toward it, touching her heart. So lovely were the sounds that she began to weep with joy. Who was playing this powerful music?

Wonder Woman flew to the open window and peered inside. A girl with dark cropped hair stood with her eyes closed, playing a violin. She looked as though she were in another world. When the music stopped, her eyes fluttered open. The girl looked directly at Wonder Woman and gasped.

"Oh, hi!" Wonder Woman said, waving. "That was beautiful. I'm Wonder Woman."

"I know who you are," the girl said, not hiding the surprise on her face. "I've been watching you on HQTV."

Wonder Woman shivered slightly. Mandy Bowin had been watching her?

"Why are you here?" the violinist asked. "Is that pie for me? I love pie."

Wonder Woman had forgotten that she was carrying the cherry pie from Buttery Bakery. "Well, yes. Then this pie is for you," she said. "I just stopped by to talk to you. You are Mandy Bowin, correct?"

The girl nodded. She looked younger than most of the kids at Super Hero High. Her face was friendly and open, her smile bright. Mandy did not look like the sort of person who would get expelled from anywhere.

"Would you like to come in?" Mandy asked. She didn't seem surprised that Wonder Woman wanted to talk to her.

"Yes, thank you," Wonder Woman said, climbing through the window.

"I'll get some plates for the pie," Mandy told her, setting her violin down. "Make yourself at home."

Wonder Woman put her lasso on the floor next to the bed, as she always did at home and in the dorm. She placed the pie on the desk and looked around. On the walls were posters of famous musicians. The shelves were crammed with music awards. Nothing seemed suspicious. On the desk was a photo of Mandy with a serious-looking man gripping a fiddle. They had the same brown eyes.

When Mandy returned, she tripped on the Lasso of Truth. Wonder Woman caught the plates and forks, but the milk flew into the air, spilling on Mandy's violin. As she lay tangled in the Lasso of Truth, Wonder Woman asked, "Are you okay?"

"I'm okay," Mandy said honestly. She had no choice. "Though it was difficult leaving Super Hero High. I'm glad Principal Waller was so great about letting me leave."

Letting her leave?

"So you weren't expelled?" Wonder Woman asked Mandy as she untangled her.

Mandy raced to her violin and blotted the spilled milk. "Expelled? No. Well . . . yes, but no. But not really. Only, just sort of. Do you know what I mean?"

Wonder Woman shook her head. Was this one of those math word problems? Was she supposed to add, then divide something?

"Can you tell me why you no longer go to Super Hero High?" she asked, handing Mandy a slice of cherry pie.

Both sat crossed-legged on the rug and began to eat.

"I never wanted to go to Super Hero High," Mandy explained with her mouth full. "Wow, this is good crust!"

Wonder Woman nodded. It was.

Mandy continued, "My dad really, really, really wanted me to be a super hero. He tried to be one when he was younger, and, well, he didn't quite make it. To make ends meet, he established himself as something of a villain . . . The Fiddler." Mandy looked at the floor when she said this. Then she took a breath and sat up straight. "Dad wanted better for me, and I did want to make him proud. So I took all the tests, aced the interview, and was accepted into the school."

Wonder Woman washed her pie down with a glass of milk, then helped herself to another slice, leaving only half of the pie in the tin. "What happened? Why did you leave?"

Mandy motioned to Wonder Woman's face. "You have a milk mustache," she said.

Wonder Woman looked in the mirror. "Oh! Yes, I do. Thank you," she said, admiring herself.

Mandy thought for a moment. "Super Hero High wasn't

for me. I never even chose a super hero name. All my life I've wanted to be a great musician. I'd rather soothe the world with my music and let someone else save it."

Wonder Woman raised her hand. "I'll save it!" she offered.

"Good!" Mandy said, smiling. "I was hoping you'd say that."

"Bumblebee said she heard you threatening Principal Waller," Wonder Woman pointed out.

Mandy began to laugh. So did Wonder Woman, though she wasn't sure why. Had she said something funny? This was good. Harley kept telling her to get a sense of humor.

"What happened was," Mandy explained, "I had a heart-to-heart with The Wall. People think she's really tough, but that's not true at all. She's really nice, only she doesn't want anyone to know. It would ruin her reputation. Waller was convinced that I had super hero potential. I know that Super Hero High is 'the' place to be. But I wanted to go to an elite music school.

"My dad would never have allowed me to leave. But if I was expelled, then he couldn't insist I stay, and the school wouldn't look bad. So Principal Waller and I staged a little argument, and I got to come home!"

Wonder Woman's mind was racing, trying to comprehend it all. "So what do you want to do?" she asked.

"I just want to create beautiful music for the world to enjoy." Mandy picked up her violin.

At Super Hero High, everyone had a weapon to thwart

evil. However, Wonder Woman noted, Mandy had an anti-weapon—something powerful, but capable of causing great happiness.

So if Mandy Bowin wasn't the person behind the threatening notes, then who was? And why was that person so anxious for her to leave Super Hero High? Wonder Woman's worry began to ramp up again, but then the strangest thing happened. Mandy closed her eyes and began to play her violin.

The music floated across the room, sweeping away Wonder Woman's worry and replacing it with joy. In that moment, she realized that she, like Mandy, needed to be who she wanted to be, and not who everyone expected her to be—especially to some unnamed bully who wanted her out.

"You are a true virtuoso, Mandy!" Wonder Woman exclaimed.

"Thank you," Mandy said without opening her eyes.

Then Wonder Woman did something she hadn't done since she had arrived at Super Hero High school. She sat back and relaxed, then closed her eyes and got lost in Mandy's beautiful music.

Dr. Arkham would have been proud.

CHAPTER 22

In the days after she had met with Mandy Bowin, Wonder Woman felt a calm she had never experienced before. Though she was still uncertain about who wanted her out of Super Hero High, the question no longer plagued her. She stopped stressing so much and instead used the extra time to focus on her super hero training. After all, soon the Super Hero High's Super Triathlon team members would be announced.

It would have been a fib for Wonder Woman to say that she didn't want to be on the team. In fact, she wanted more than anything to represent her school in the competition. In every class Wonder Woman focused as hard as she could, asking questions, listening, taking notes. She honed her skills with her lasso, bracelets, and tiara. Wonder Woman worked and worked, and when she got tired, she rested, recharged, and worked some more. She was so exhausted at night, she slept soundly. She didn't even hear Harley telling jokes and laughing at herself in her sleep.

Wonder Woman stopped watching the HQTV videos of herself and reading the comments. The only emails she opened were from her mother, and when an anonymous note was left for her, she handed it over to Hawkgirl or Lois, not bothering to read it.

Although she was tired, Wonder Woman had no problem getting up the morning of the team announcement. An assembly was scheduled, one that would change the lives of four of the students in the room. It usually took a couple of minutes for everyone to settle down. But on this day, no one was flying around or floating above their seats. No, everyone was where they should be and facing forward.

Onstage, the teachers sat on oversized thrones—Crazy Quilt's idea—behind Principal Waller.

"Today we announce the members of Team Super Hero High," The Wall began. The only sound in the auditorium was an infinitesimally tiny ping caused by a minor computer malfunction in Cyborg's titanium circuitry system. "This designation is a high honor. Not only will those called represent the school, but their actions will be on display for the entire world, and beyond, to see.

"Team Super Hero High members, when I call your name, please join me on this stage," Principal Waller said. There was a discernible shift in the auditorium air as she held up a sealed envelope. "Even I have not seen this final list yet."

Wonder Woman could barely breathe.

"The first member of Team Super Hero High is . . ."

Wonder Woman leaned forward.

"Katana!"

The auditorium erupted in cheers. Doing cartwheels and landing on the stage, Katana gave Principal Waller a deep bow before doing the same to the teachers and then to the audience.

Wonder Woman clapped wildly for her friend, then sat down. There were three more team members, plus the alternate.

"Will Frost, please join us!" The Wall said.

The temperature dropped when Frost stood tall, surveying the audience. Wonder Woman thought she saw the hint of a warm smile on Frost's face.

"And now, will Beast Boy make his way up here, please!" Principal Waller called out.

Shape-shifting from a boy to an elephant to a German shepherd to a gazelle, with several other animals in between, Beast Boy raised both arms in victory and blew kisses to the audience.

There was only one spot left on the team. Who would it be? Wonder Woman could hardly sit still. She looked around. Harley was bouncing up and down in her seat. Poison Ivy was twirling her long ginger locks. Bumblebee had gone from girl-sized to bee-sized and back again. Green Lantern was cracking his knuckles, and Cheetah looked miffed.

"The fourth member of Team Super Hero High is . . ."

Wonder Woman closed her eyes. She remembered how

embarrassing it was when she thought she had been named Hero of the Month and stood up when Poison Ivy's name had been called. She wanted to be sure not to make that mistake again.

Wonder Woman recalled her first day at Super Hero High, in this very auditorium, when she tripped while heading to the stage. That was only a couple of months ago. So much had happened since then, and . . .

"Wonder Woman!" Principal Waller said—again.

Wha . . . ?

"Wonder Woman, are you just going to sit there, or will you be joining your teammates on the stage?"

Huh?

"Go, Wondy, go!" Bumblebee said, pushing her up from her seat and down the aisle.

As she stood with the other members of Team Super Hero High, Wonder Woman could not believe she was there. Harley was videotaping.

"Hi, Mom!" Wonder Woman called to the camera. She almost added, "Hi, Mandy!" but caught herself, and instead said, "Hi, Virtuoso!" knowing that her new friend was watching and would understand the code name. Wonder Woman's heart was about to burst with pride.

"We aren't quite done yet," Principal Waller said, clearing her throat. "These talented super heroes you see standing in front of you were selected not only for their individual talents, but for how their skills and powers complement each other's. The final member of the team is an alternate. However, that person's role is no less challenging. That's because as an alternate, they must be able to step in at any time, taking over if one of the other team members cannot compete for any reason. Not only must the alternate have their own unique powers, but they have to be able to adapt their skills and abilities to the team's."

Wonder Woman looked out at the audience. Everyone was sitting still. "Our Team Super Hero High alternate is . . ."

Who would it be? Wonder Woman searched the crowd.

"Hawkgirl!" Waller called out.

The second her friend stepped onstage, Wonder Woman rushed over to hug her. Hawkgirl seemed to be in shock.

"Congratulations to all these fine young super heroes," Waller said. "And to all of you. Each and every one of you has powers that you may not even be aware of yet. Though you are not on the Super Triathlon team, you are all part of the team here at Super Hero High, and together we will strive to make the world a better place."

After the assembly, the coaches let the team members jump up and down, bounce off the buildings, fly through the clouds, slice things up, and run around the world—before asking them to meet in the gym.

Without regular classes, the team had one month to focus

on training for the Super Triathlon. Star Sapphire, whose costume in Crazy Quilt's class had earned her an A+, was put in charge of the team uniforms, and Bumblebee was named weapons/equipment manager. Harley, of course, was team videographer.

Even though she wasn't on Team Super Hero High, it seemed to Wonder Woman that wherever she went, whatever she did, Cheetah was always right there.

"It should have been me instead of you," she hissed, motioning to her bandaged leg. Others were always around, too, such as Barbara Gordon, the team statistician. Lois Lane was doing a Web series called *The High Price of Competition*, featuring team members not only from Super Hero High, but from other top-ranked schools as well. And the Riddler kept showing up and joking constantly that he was the alternate's alternate. Hawkgirl didn't find it funny.

The students had always been closely watched, but now they were really put under a microscope. The public couldn't get enough about the private lives, or, as Harley called her series, *Super Secret Lives*, of teen super heroes.

The weeks flew by. All the teammates had their challenges. Beast Boy refused to double-check his work. Liberty Belle, who was in charge of the academic portion, had to keep telling him to slow down.

When it came time for the on-the-spot super hero interview, Frost had to be coached not to freeze out the judges. During the practice A/P test, which counted for a full 50 percent in prelims, Katana was so eager to show off her skills that she would whip out unregistered swords and knives. Bumblebee had to keep a special watch on her lest she cause the whole team to get penalized.

The only person who was stellar in all three categories was Wonder Woman.

"Hey, I've heard that a new super hero might be joining the student body soon," Lois said as she took notes on everyone's progress. "Know anything about it?"

Hawkgirl stopped doing pushups. "I've heard a rumor that they're from another planet."

"That would be great," Wonder Woman noted. "It would be fun to learn a lot from someone different." As it was, Wonder Woman was learning how to be a triathlete. Soon she would find out if she'd succeed. The one hundredth Super Triathlon competition was looming.

CHAPTER 23

As mysteriously as the threats had started, they stopped. It had been several days since Wonder Woman had received one.

"I hope it's over with," Hawkgirl said.

"Many times if you don't engage with the bad guys, they back off," Lois Lane informed her. "I've done several articles about this, and generally villains are lashing out to try to get even for something that has happened to them. They're cowards, really."

"I may never know who it was, but I'm glad it seems to have stopped," Wonder Woman said, letting out a sigh of relief.

Star Sapphire stood in front of the team with five mannequins, each covered with a blue cloth. "These," she said, "are your Super Triathlon uniforms. I've taken each of your current super hero costumes and modified them, adding a Team

Super Hero High logo and other embellishments to create a cohesive look.

"This past week, I've worked with Crazy Quilt and the Super Sewing Club to make these. If any of you has a problem with what I've done, then too bad. It's too late. However," she said, toying with her Violet Lantern ring and flashing an irresistible smile, "I'm sure you will love what I have done."

With that, she pulled on a rope and the blue cloths were yanked up, revealing the uniforms. There was an audible gasp from the team.

"Star Sapphire, these are incredible!" Wonder Woman said. "These really complete us. Thank you!"

Star Sapphire smiled. "You're welcome, Wonder Woman," she said. "Anything for the team!"

Wildcat had taken on the role of head athletic coach for the triathlon. As he stood before the team with his blue SHH baseball cap worn backward, he reviewed the stats and analysis of each competitor, which Barbara Gordon had created with a computer program she'd developed herself. Wildcat nodded several times as he flipped through the pages. Sometimes he smiled. Other times, he frowned. Once, he laughed out loud.

"Your attention, please!" he called.

Katana sheathed her sword. Beast Boy turned human.

Frost chilled out. Hawkgirl stood at attention. Wonder Woman coiled her lasso.

"You all have been putting in a two-hundred percent effort. As has our support team of Bumblebee, Star Sapphire, and Barbara," he added. "But now is the time for one of you to step forward and assume your role as Team Captain. As such, it will be your job to lead and encourage the team— Yes, Wonder Woman, did you have a question?"

Wonder Woman put her hand down and shook her head. She had merely been volunteering to be Team Captain.

"Those of you who would like to be considered for this prestigious position— Yes, Wonder Woman, did you have a question?

Wonder Woman put her hand down and shook her head again. Again, she'd wanted to volunteer to be Team Captain.

"Ahem," Wildcat said, taking off his SHH baseball cap and scratching his head. "As I was saying, if you'd like to be considered, then we would like to hear from you now."

The team members looked at each other, and then stood up. Wonder Woman looked around and stood up, too.

"Good!" Wildcat noted. "You all are leaders. However, we are looking for a leader among leaders. Who would like to speak first? Tell us why you are suited for this role, and then, as a group, we will elect our team captain."

Katana went first. "I can cut through any problem," she promised, wielding her sword.

"As your team captain, I promise the other schools won't

know what's happening!" Beast Boy said, morphing into a dozen creatures in less than ten seconds.

"I'll stay cool under pressure," Frost said as she made it rain icicles.

"Wonder Woman," Wildcat said. "Your turn."

Wonder Woman stood before her coaches and peers. She thought about what her mother had told her, that she was an ambassador for Paradise Island. And now she was lobbying to be an ambassador for Super Hero High on the world stage.

"It would be an honor to lead this team to victory," Wonder Woman began. Frost's eyes narrowed. Beast Boy turned into a monkey and began scratching his armpit. Katana sharpened her blade. Wonder Woman noticed Cheetah lurking behind a tree.

She continued, "Each of us has powers, abilities, and enormous potential, but none of us is as powerful individually as we are as a team. The Super Triathlon is a team competition. This is not for personal glory, but to showcase what the students of Super Hero High can do when we pull together.

"I know that some of you have been told in the past what you can't do. Well, I am here to tell you what you *can* do. You can embrace your inner super hero. Fly higher, run faster, fight harder, think smarter. We can do this together. We are Team Super Hero High, and if I am chosen to be your team captain, I promise to do everything in my power to make it happen. Because I believe in you. I believe in us."

The last week rushed by in a blur. As Team Captain, Wonder Woman made sure not only that everyone trained hard, but that they stopped to relax and recharge, too.

"This music is great," Katana said as she leaned against a tree and sliced Poison Apples for the team. "It's really powerful. Who is this?"

"It's an up-and-coming musician called Virtuoso," Wonder Woman said, smiling at the thought of Mandy playing the violin in her room.

Just then, Principal Waller walked up to the team. "Sit back down," she told them. "I'm just here to tell you how much I appreciate the hard work you've all been putting in. Tomorrow morning, we march into the LexCorp Super Triathlon Arena, and tomorrow night we will know which school takes home the championship title.

"Whatever the outcome," Principal Waller said, "you are already winners. I want you to know that. You know that I don't give out much praise"—everyone nodded in agreement, even the teachers—"so when I do, I mean it. And I mean it when I tell you that I am proud of each and every one of you. You are all great reflections of Super Hero High. Get a good night's rest, and good luck. Tomorrow will be a big day."

CHAPTER 24

Buses, cars, airplanes, jet packs, and even some old-school spacecraft poured into the parking lot adjacent to the massive LexCorp Super Triathlon Arena.

As they made their way to the tunnels under the arena, some teams looked nervous, and others looked angry. Wonder Woman and the rest of her team felt calm and confident in their uniforms designed by Star Sapphire. Star Sapphire herself was wearing a team jacket over her costume, and so was her assistant, Golden Glider, who was dressed in a LIVE T-shirt and a shimmering skirt that matched her skates. Bumblebee had on a new warm-up suit with the school logo on the back. All needed to be comfortable in their supporting roles. And even though Hawkgirl was an alternate, she was in full competition gear, ready to jump in at a moment's notice.

The CAD Academy team, clad in red metallic uniforms, brushed by them. Captain Cold sneered at Star Sapphire and stared down Golden Glider, then accidentally-on-purpose shoved Bumblebee. The spare weapons Bumblebee was carrying spilled onto the ground.

"Hey!" she yelled at Captain Cold as Heat Wave and Ratcatcher laughed. "Not cool!"

"Not cool?" Heat Wave asked. "Okay, let's heat things up, shall we?"

Before he could ignite a fight, Katana brandished her sword.

"Stop it, Heat Wave," the only girl on the CAD Academy team ordered.

"Why, Magpie?" Heat Wave whined. "I got this."

"We'll settle this on the field," she said. Her lips curled up into an evil grin.

Wonder Woman stepped between the two. "Save it for the competition, Katana," she told her friend. "If you lose your temper, we could all get disqualified."

Her eyes flashing, Katana put her sword down. "No one hurts my friends," she said through gritted teeth. "I'll see you in the arena!" she called to the CAD Academy team.

Ratcatcher had already knocked someone over from Stalwart Secondary, and the rest of the team were now mocking the mascot from Pluto Prep, chanting, "Live evil!"

Just then Harley ran up, her video camera in hand. The red Record light was blinking. "Did I miss a conflict?" When no one answered, she turned the camera on her roommate.

"Wonder Woman, in less than an hour, you will lead Super Hero High in competition against the top teams in the universe. How do you feel?"

"I feel great," Wonder Woman said, looking straight at the camera, as Harley had taught her to do.

"Anything you want to say to the other schools?" Harley asked.

"Yes!" Wonder Woman nodded. "To all of our competitors, *including Team CAD Academy,* I wish you all good luck! Let's have a fun and fair Super Triathlon!"

"You meant that, didn't you?" Lois Lane asked Wonder Woman as Harley left to chase down a rumor that Superman had made an appearance. He had competed in the Super Triathlon when he was at Super Hero High.

Wonder Woman nodded. "Of course."

"Thought so," Lois said. "I need a quote for you for Super News. But first I have something for you."

Wonder Woman froze as Lois held out a note. She had almost forgotten that someone wanted to see her fail.

"Open it," Lois encouraged. She didn't look upset.

Slowly, Wonder Woman unfolded the paper. The writing was in neat block letters. As she read it, her smile grew. It said:

Best of luck, Wondy. I hope you and the team do well. I'm rooting for you! I couldn't get out of work, but I'll be watching on TV. Win or lose, come into the

Capes & Cowls Cafe for a free smoothie, my treat!
—Steve (Trevor) from Capes & Cowls Cafe, the boy
with the braces

While Wonder Woman's team warmed up in their state-of-the-art locker room and control center, they couldn't help looking at the bank of TV monitors that lined the walls. A Who's Who of super heroes strolled, rolled, and flew down the red carpet on their way to the VIP (Very Important Paragons) skyboxes that floated above the LexCorp Arena. Rival TV and Web channels jostled to get the best interviews, but none of them were as aggressive, or as successful, as Harley Quinn of HQTV.

Harley was interviewing the ultimate hero of modern times, Superman. "Well, of course I'll be cheering for my alma mater, Super Hero High," he said. "I've heard that this year's team is one of the best ever."

Wonder Woman felt warm inside. And it wasn't just from the relentless abdominal presses Wildcat had made the team do, or the leg stretches she was doing now. She stopped suddenly and looked up when she heard a familiar voice.

"My name is Hippolyta, and I am Queen of the Amazon warriors from Paradise Island."

"Which team will you be rooting for?" Harley asked. "And why?"

"Team Super Hero High, of course," Hippolyta said, as if that were a silly question. "My daughter, Wonder Woman, is the Team Captain, and I am so proud of her. She has proven to me that she is living her own life and doing a great job of it. She is my role model."

Wonder Woman felt a lump in her throat. But before it got her all choked up, Wildcat yelled, "LET'S GO! Team Super Hero High, line up for the march of the super heroes. Our time is now!"

The elaborate opening ceremony at the Super Triathlon exceeded Wonder Woman's dreams. Of course, it was to be expected, with this being the hundred-year anniversary of the event. As Wonder Woman and her team swept into the LexCorp Arena, the All-Stars Symphony played the majestic strains of "Victors' Theme," the official song of the Super Triathlon. Wonder Woman, Katana, Beast Boy, and Frost were met with a roar from the crowd. All waved in practiced unison before taking their seats on the green marble dais that occupied the center of field.

The arena was huge, and for spectators and super heroes in the audience who did not have super-vision, giant videos were projected into the sky. Enterprising merchants were hawking souvenir Super de Duper Eye Goggles at a buy two, get one free discount. School merchandise ranging from plastic shields, capes, masks, and the ever-popular energy juice bottles were also selling swiftly. T-shirts featuring individual competitors in heroic poses were everywhere.

The competition was being broadcast live by all the major networks and streamed to more than two dozen planets. Plus, of course, there were upstarts like HQTV, who in several short months had become the go-to Web channel for everything about super hero teens.

Because it was boring to watch teenage super heroes take written exams during the academic portion of the competition, the organizers had set up a karaoke contest featuring audience members. Karaoke prelims had taken place prior to the Super Triathlon, and the finals were being held live. In a crowd-pleasing twist, all finalists were duos. On the stage stood Black Orchid and Firestorm, Thunder and Lightning, and crowd favorites Green Arrow and Black Canary.

Wonder Woman could hear the strains of music seeping under the door in the Quiet Quiz Room, where the teams were taking their exams. Liberty Belle had prepped her team well in the facts, fiction, and legends of super hero history. However, everyone knew that the team from Interstellar Magnet had the inside track on the academic portion of the competition. Wonder Woman flexed her muscles, then tackled the test.

★

After the papers were handed in, nine of the fifty teams were disqualified for cheating—mind reading was not allowed in the test room. The remaining forty-one teams were sent to the Interview Station to test their public relations mettle. Every super hero knew that how they presented themselves in public was part of their legacy and lore. You could be a great super hero, but if you mumbled or muddled your way through an interview, your popularity might plummet.

Each team member was interviewed independently, though all were asked the same questions:

1. Why do you want to be a super hero?

2. How can you make a difference in the world?

3. If you were a tree, what kind would you be?

4. Who is your favorite super hero, and why?

When it was Wonder Woman's turn, she remembered to smile, introduce herself, and shake each of the judge's hands.

"I don't just want to be a super hero," she said. "I *need* to be one. It is part of who I am and my destiny."

"My goal is to help rid the world of evil and bring about peace."

"Oak."

"My mother."

Going into the last event of the prelims, CAD Academy was in the lead, having nailed the interviews. Their arrogance seemed like confidence to the judges. As expected, Interstellar Magnet won the academic section. Super Hero High had come in sixth in Academic, and a decent fourth in

Interview. They would have been higher, but Wonder Woman had accidentally squeezed too hard when shaking one of the interview judges' hands, causing him to yell, "I surrender!" as the audience roared with laughter. Luckily, Super Hero High's strongest event was up next: Abilities/Powers, also known as the A/P test. Because it counted for 50 percent of the prelim score, expectation and tension were high in the LexCorp Arena.

CHAPTER 25

The preliminary round went quickly. It netted ten teams that moved up to the semifinals, including three-time champion Intensity Institute. Few were surprised by the prelim results, for as the old saying goes, "A strong meteor shower separates the flyers from the fallers."

The other schools in contention were, in no particular order, Wheeler-Nicholson Prep, CAD Academy, Powers Alternative Education, Cavalier Community School, Interstellar Magnet, Stalwart Secondary, Foundation for the Telepathic and Telekinetic Talented & Gifted, Super Hero High, and a controversial ad hoc team of upstart homeschooled super heroes from a small suburb on the planet Bismol, who went by the symbol

Round two, the semifinals, ramped up the competition. This time, Interview counted for 10 percent, Academics for

20 percent, and the all-important A/P test made up the rest with a whopping 70 percent. The competition was fierce, and in the end three teams were disqualified and two were wiped out, clearly out of their league. Many had scrapes to their bodies and their egos, and the coach of Intensity Institute threw a hurricane-force hissy fit before demanding a recount.

"And now, representing their schools in the final and most challenging round of the one hundredth annual Super Triathlon are . . . ," the Unseen Voice boomed across the LexCorp Arena, "CAD Academy, Interstellar Magnet, and . . ."–Wonder Woman held her breath–"Super Hero High!"

As the audience went wild, the team from Wheeler-Nicholson Prep threw down their weapons in protest and stomped on them. Then a clot of unruly parents from Cavalier Community School started a fight in the stands and had to be forcibly removed from the stadium.

Amidst the commotion and congratulations, the finalists took the stage. Ratcatcher, Magpie, and Heat Wave from CAD Academy oozed confidence as Captain Cold led them in a bow, his ice-blue eyes locking on Wonder Woman as he smirked.

Interstellar Magnet looked like they were in shock, and Team Super Hero High hugged and waved to their family and friends, who were all sitting together in the stands, cheering.

Soon the flashy halftime show was under way, featuring "the unique smilin' 'n' stylin' of ultra-famous superstar singer Enchantress! and her 777 backup dancers."

As she cast her spell on the crowd, the competitors returned to the locker rooms to recharge. In this last and most important segment of the competition, the scoreboard was wiped clean. Academics and Interview was no longer part of the event. Now it all came down to the A/P test.

No one knew what was ahead, only that they would be tested like never before. One year, the teams were sent to uncharted distant planets and charged with pushing their gravitational rotations in the opposite direction. Another year, it came down to a simple race around the world, albeit through a meteor shower and other crowd-pleasing disasters. What would it be this time?

"Wondy, a few words?" Wildcat said.

Huh? Wonder Woman looked up. Her team was waiting for her to speak. Bumblebee was checking the weapons for the umpteenth time, and Star Sapphire and Golden Glider were taking inventory of the uniforms. Cheetah stopped by to drop off some energy drinks.

Wonder Woman stood up and faced her teammates. "You all are amazing," she began. "Though our training has been tough, it has brought us together. Katana, Frost, Beast Boy, and Hawkgirl, I am so proud of you. Win or lose, or anything in between, you have brought honor to Team Super Hero High, and I thank you. Now let's go out there and show them what we're made of!"

Bumblebee took her role as Weapons Manager very

seriously. As each competitor marched past, she handed them their weapons or checked their powers. A freshly sharpened sword for Katana, buffed and polished bracelets and tiara for Wonder Woman, along with her tightly coiled lasso. Beast Boy's and Frost's weapons were themselves—their innate abilities to draw from within to defend or attack. Bumblebee had Beast Boy turn into five creatures in ten seconds and made sure Frost could freeze a fire before allowing them to proceed.

Hawkgirl, the alternate team member, was outfitted with her newly upgraded Nth Metal belt, which granted her the power of flight, and enhanced her strength and sight.

Once all were cleared by Bumblebee, they passed by Star Sapphire, who ensured that their costumes were all in order, checking that Wonder Woman's lasso was securely attached and her bracelets were on the correct arms as Golden Glider's ice-blue eyes double-checked for any rips.

Team Super Hero High was now ready for the final competition. Everything was in its proper place. Or was it? As the team marched into the arena, Wonder Woman thought she saw Cheetah slip into the shadows.

There was a roar of approval as the finalists made their way onto the stage. Wonder Woman and Interstellar Magnet's Team Captain, Kanjar Ro, nodded to each other, while

Captain Cold from CAD Academy refused to look at anyone, preferring to act bored.

"How do you think our competitors will do?" Katana whispered to Wonder Woman.

"I have no idea," she said. "But don't let yourself get distracted by that. Instead of focusing on them, let's focus on what we can do."

The crowd gasped as the giant black tent was lifted by several state-of-the art prototype Ferris Aircraft spacecraft. Before them was a floating model of Earth that expanded as it levitated, rising above the LexCorp Arena.

The Unseen Announcer allowed the crowd to settle down. "In this year's competition," he began, "our young super heroes will be battling the elements: land, air, fire, and water. The team scores will be tallied, and the one with the most points will be declared the one hundredth Super Triathlon champion. Plus, we will name an individual Super Triathlete of the games. Are we ready to superpower through this?"

The crowd cheered.

"What? I can't hear you!" the Unseen Announcer teased.

A roar shook the arena. It seemed so loud that some of the lesser planets might have actually realigned.

"That's the spirit! Now, finalists, you know this, but I will say it one more time. Not only are you allowed to use your weapons and powers, you are expected to. However, you may not use them on your fellow competitors. Injuries will result in an immediate point deduction and possible disqualification. Understood?"

All the competitors nodded, though a couple of super heroes from CAD Academy could be seen sneering. "Live evil!" Captain Cold hissed so softly that only Wonder Woman could hear him.

"Good!" the Unseen Announcer said. "There are four events, beginning with land. Within each challenge, the teams will be scored on the four Ss of Superdom: strategy, speed, strength, and skills. Now . . . let's find out who our champions will be!"

CHAPTER 26

The first A/P Test seemed pretty basic—the teen super heroes were charged with moving something. This final phase of the competition always began this way. In past years, teams moved towering blocks of granite awash in grease, a mega cruise ship buried in the sand, and a massive fleet of monster trucks. Wonder Woman had heard via HQTV's new *Hearsay Everyday* gossip hotline that they would be moving a mountain. That made sense—the earth portion of the test was up first.

"I'm ready! I'm ready!" Beast Boy chanted eagerly.

Frost shot him a chilly glare and Katana shushed him so they could hear the Unseen Announcer. "You will be moving . . ." However, instead of saying, "a mountain," the Unseen Announcer said, ". . . a MOLEHILL!!!"

Ultra-bright spotlights hit the center of the arena. When Team Super Hero High saw the little pile of dirt with their name next to it, they were perplexed. Interstellar Magnet huddled together and whispered, while Team CAD Academy laughed.

"Super Triathletes," the Unseen Announcer boomed, "you will move a molehill from point A to point B and leave not a single speck of dirt behind." Two hundred feet away hung a large letter "B" with an arrow pointing down at a ten-foot circle of chromium, the world's hardest metal.

The Unseen Announcer continued. "Team Captains, raise your hands if you understand. Thank you. Now let's get these games started, shall we?"

Wonder Woman put on her game face, focusing on the task ahead. Magpie from CAD Academy grabbed the molehill, but as he held an armful of dirt, another molehill popped up in its place. When Maxima from Interstellar Magnet tried to push their molehill, it fell apart, scattering dirt everywhere.

Team Super Hero High stared at their molehill. Wonder Woman bent down and picked up a handful of dirt. Instantly, more dirt flew up from the ground, replacing it. She stared at the fresh dirt and said, "Beast Boy, can you turn into a mole and tell me what's happening underground?"

"Sure thing!" Seconds later, Beast Boy emerged from the molehill. "The moles aren't very happy about this," he reported. "They take great pride in their work. They don't want anyone touching their molehills."

"Then why are they doing this?" Katana asked.

"They were promised a year's worth of gourmet grubs and an annual subscription to *Tunnel Talk* magazine to participate," Beast Boy explained to the team.

Wonder Woman nodded. *Tunnel Talk* was an excellent periodical. "I have a plan," she announced. "Here's what we're going to do. . . ."

Wonder Woman placed the dirt back onto the ground, while two hundred feet away at point B, Katana used the flat side of her sword to loosen the heavy chromium plate from where it was anchored. Once Katana got it on its side, Wonder Woman could use her Lasso of Truth to move the two-ton chromium, revealing a fresh patch of soil. Meanwhile, Beast Boy returned underground to talk to the moles again, and Frost used her powers to create a fun, perfectly mole-sized ice tunnel slide for them to rush toward point B. There, under the arrow, the dirt flew as Team Super Hero High cheered on the moles creating a lovely molehill.

"The first round goes to . . . , " the Unseen Announcer said, "CAD Academy!" Surprised, Wonder Woman looked over at her competition. Their molehill sat atop the chromium circle . . . along with a family of angry moles who had been bullied into building a molehill with displaced dirt.

Captain Cold smiled at Wonder Woman and shook his head. "Oops, you lost," he said with faux sadness. Then his team broke out laughing and congratulated themselves, as their moles chirped bitterly and squinted under the bright lights.

"In the next event of the one hundredth Super Triathlon, our young elite super heroes will be up against fire!" the Unseen Announcer told the crowd.

As the teams took their places onstage, Maxima from Interstellar Magnet was looking particularly glum. Her team was in a distant third place. With CAD Academy in first place, Captain Cold was even more smug than usual. Team Super Hero High was solidly in second place, and would have been even closer had they just displaced the moles instead of working with them. But it was important to Wonder Woman and her team to respect everyone. Besides, it was just the first challenge of the A/P Test. They could make up the points in the coming events.

Wonder Woman waved to her mom, who was sitting in the parent block of the Super Hero High cheering section, then focused on the announcer.

"For fire, teams will take their places on the field. In each team's designated area is a bunker of unlit fireworks. Fire Trolls are standing by to lob fireballs. Their goal is to ignite the fireworks. If any team's fireworks explode while the clock is counting down, that team loses the fire challenge. If no fireworks are lit, then the number of fireballs destroyed or lobbed back at the trolls counts for points.

"Super heroes, take your places!"

As her team marched to their area, Wonder Woman noticed Frost and Captain Cold glaring at each other.

"Don't do it!" Wonder Woman cautioned.

"Do what?" Frost asked.

"Use your powers on him. That would be a mandatory point deduction for us and could even get you disqualified."

"He thinks he's so great," Frost said coolly. "Sure, he can make things cold, but I can freeze them."

"We're all counting on that," Wonder Woman told her.

As they took their places around their fireworks bunker, Katana readied her sword, Frost braced herself, Wonder Woman adjusted her bracelets, and, to the crowd's delight, Beast Boy turned into a dragon.

The Fire Trolls slogged their way into the arena, and the crowd gasped. They were rarely seen in public, and the last confirmed sighting had been years earlier. Since then, they had gained weight and looked out of shape. Yet one should never underestimate a true villain. These hulking red creatures dripping with lava seldom came out from beneath their volcanoes. But, as the Unseen Announcer explained, "In the spirit of the one hundredth Super Triathlon, everyone is eager to play their role in history."

The fireballs started slowly, with only a few at first, but that was just a warm-up. Katana leapt and whirled, using her sword to slice each fireball into a thousand embers that glowed bright orange before disintegrating. Wonder Woman used her bracelets to deflect fireballs and send them flying into the atmosphere, and Frost froze the fireballs in midair, watching as the ice melted and steam rose from where fire once was. But it was Beast Boy who wowed the crowd.

As a fire-breathing dragon, he fought fire with fire. One roar could emit a fifty-foot flame that knocked the wind out of the Fire Trolls' cantaloupe-sized projectiles. Soon the trolls teamed up to bring Beast Boy down.

"Frost! Now!" Wonder Woman ordered.

Katana ran to Beast Boy's side as Frost began blanketing the firework bunker with sheets of ice to render them unusable. Looking over at the CAD Academy team, Frost accidentally-on-purpose sent an icicle missile aimed at Captain Cold. He intercepted it with a blast of cold, sending it back and knocking her over.

"Stop goofing off and get up!" Wonder Woman yelled at Frost. "Katana is in trouble!"

There was no time to finish icing the fireworks. Katana's sword was on fire! How could that be? It was made from the strongest metal on earth. But there it was, in flames. Frost quickly put out the fire with a blast of ice, leaving Beast Boy to battle the Fire Trolls alone. Suddenly, there was an explosion. The blast lit up the sky in a rainbow of colors as CAD Academy's fireworks bunker ignited. Beast Boy turned to see the explosion, and a fireball swept past him. In an instant, Team Super Hero High's fireworks bunker exploded, too.

By default, Interstellar Magnet won the round and were suddenly back in the game.

CHAPTER 27

Wildcat was trying to calm Bumblebee down. She was in a tizzy. As weapons manager, it was Bumblebee's job to make sure everything was in working order.

"Who did this?" Katana demanded. "Someone will pay for sabotaging my sword!"

"I don't know," Bumblebee said, flying circles around the locker room, on the verge of tears. "I have your backup swords right here."

Beast Boy looked up, having guzzled several gallons of water. Being a fire-breathing dragon was exhausting. "Maybe someone doesn't like you," he said.

"Maybe *I* don't like *you*," Katana shot back.

"Is there anything I can do?" Hawkgirl asked as she paced the room.

"It wasn't you, was it?" Katana said, her eyes narrowing. "You're the alternate, and if I'm out, then you're in!"

Hawkgirl looked shocked. Before she could answer,

Wonder Woman stepped between them.

"She didn't do it," Wonder Woman said. "Hawkgirl would never do something like that. Katana, I am so sorry your sword was sabotaged, but we don't have time to dwell on it right now. Our next competition is up."

Katana did a side kick, deliberately knocking over a trash can. "I'm sorry," she told Hawkgirl. "And sorry to you, too, Beast Boy," she said, clenching her fists. "It's just that I want to win so badly."

"We all do," Star Sapphire said. She looked over everyone's uniforms as Golden Glider expertly mended the torn parts.

"Let's go!" Wildcat shouted. He pulled Wonder Woman over. "We'll get to the bottom of this later. If someone tampered with Katana's sword, that's serious business. I'll make sure Bumblebee keeps an eye on the weapons. And for extra security, I'll have Star Sapphire help her."

The deep-water challenge took a lot of strategy. With no aqua members on any of the teams, they were all forced to make do. However, Team Super Hero High had the advantage of Beast Boy's ability to shape-shift. Wonder Woman was glad that when she was little, her mother had forced her to take swimming lessons, even though she didn't like putting her face underwater.

There were three chests at the bottom of the sea, but

only one held treasure. Whichever team was able to bring it to the surface would win. But the chests were guarded by armies of Eclectic Electric Eels—that is, eels of various sizes and hues with the ability to electrify anyone who came in contact with them. The teams were flown by a Ferris Aircraft to a remote ocean and dropped from a thousand feet in the sky as camera-equipped drones broadcast from above the water. The prototype Ferris Aquatic Camera Cars videoed from below.

The battle was brutal. The Eclectic Electric Eels took too much delight in shocking the competitors, who had to constantly come up for air. As the Super Hero High team swam toward the treasure chest, Katana released her sword, letting it float to the bottom of the ocean. Beast Boy shook his head. Wonder Woman motioned for them all to surface. When they did, Katana explained, "The eels are drawn to metal. If you have anything metal on you, get rid of it."

Wonder Woman took off her bracelets as she and Frost hitched a ride on Beast Boy, who had morphed into a giant sea turtle. Free from the Eclectic Electric Eel attacks, they made it to the three treasure chests before the other teams. Beast Boy—who was now a massive blue whale—blocked the other competitors. Wonder Woman dived to the ocean floor and retrieved the treasure chest. She opened it to find that it was full of gold coins, but instantly, the eels were alerted. In one sweeping gesture, she dumped the coins out, then pushed off from the ocean's floor with such force that she shot out of the water. Once in the sky, she kept flying all the way back to the LexCorp Arena as her teammates followed.

"Why did you dump the treasure?" Harley Quinn yelled as the triumphant team walked toward the locker room, leaving puddles behind them. Beast Boy kept blowing water out his nose.

Wonder Woman tilted her head to the side and hit it to try to get the water out of her ear. "The task was to bring back the treasure chest, but not necessarily the treasure," Wonder Woman explained.

Bumblebee was still buzzing in circles when the team entered the locker room.

"What's the matter?" Wonder Woman asked. Bumblebee was on the verge of tears as she returned to her full size. "What is it?" she asked gently.

"Your lasso—it's missing!" Bumblebee blurted before getting small again.

Wonder Woman froze. How could that be? Wonder Woman had left it in the locker room for safety, knowing she couldn't use it underwater. But now it was gone? First Katana's sword was compromised, and now her lasso was missing!

"Star Sapphire," Wonder Woman called, "my lasso has disappeared, and . . ." Before she could finish her sentence, Wonder Woman was relieved to see Golden Glider at the far end of the locker room holding the Lasso of Truth. "You found it!"

Before Golden Glider could respond, Cheetah appeared from nowhere. Golden Glider tried desperately to skate away, but Cheetah was faster. She lunged for the lasso, wrenching it from Golden Glider's hands and growling, "Give it up!"

As Cheetah was about to run off with the lasso, Bumblebee flew in and grabbed it, delivering it safely to Wonder Woman's hands.

"Cheetah?" Wonder Woman gasped, confused.

"I—," Cheetah started to say.

"Team Super Hero High, on the stage NOW," Wildcat ordered. "We will deal with this when the competition is over."

"Cheetah?" Wonder Woman said again as she left the locker room.

"You don't understand," Cheetah said defiantly. "You just don't get it."

As they made their way to the stage, Katana whispered to Wonder Woman, "She's had it in for you ever since you knocked her over and she hurt her leg. Cheetah's gone around telling everyone that you stole her spot on the team."

Wonder Woman shook her head. "It was an accident," she insisted. "Does she hate me that much?"

The official music started playing, and all the teams faced the audience as the Unseen Announcer began. "There is currently a tie between CAD Academy and Super Hero High. This final event will determine the winner of the one hundredth Super Triathlon."

The crowd shifted anxiously. Wonder Woman waved to Hippolyta, who was holding up her **GO, WONDER WOMAN!** sign and wearing a Wonder Woman T-shirt. Next to her, Hawkgirl's grandmother held a **TEAM SHHS** banner. *Too bad she can't see her beloved granddaughter in competition,* Wonder Woman thought.

"This final event harkens back to old-fashioned picnic games, with a super hero *twist,*" the Unseen Announcer declared.

This last event of the competition took place in the center of the arena. The anticipation was high, and the spectators could barely contain their excitement. Several elementary- and middle-school super heroes were put in a time-out, and many famous super hero parents were reminded that they were role models and were asked to calm down.

As the referees passed out burlap sacks, the competitors looked confused.

"The sacks are for you to wear," the Unseen Announcer began. Impatient to begin the competition, Ratcatcher and Beast Boy put the sacks on their heads. Wonder Woman and her team waited to hear whether the sacks would self-destruct, squeeze them into incapacitation, or perhaps emit a rash-causing poison. All were surprised to hear, "You step into them, and then you hop to the finish line! No flying, shape-shifting, or teleporting is allowed on the ground. Only jumping."

"This stinks!" muttered Magpie as her teammates

nodded. "Who do they think we are, average mortals?"

About a mile away, another referee waved and pointed to the end of the race, one foot away from the edge of a cliff.

The Unseen Announcer explained, "You must stop at the end, and anything past that disqualifies you. If you find yourself falling off the cliff, you may use your superpowers to rescue yourself or your teammates, should that be necessary. Got it? Good. Ready? On your marks, get set, go!"

Laughter swept through the stands as the audience watched some of the best young super heroes in history hopping up and down in burlap sacks. It looked awkward and easy at the same time. Just when Wonder Woman was getting the hang of it, she felt the wind change.

"All eyes to the west!" she yelled to her teammates. Headed straight toward them was a massive supercell formation— twin tornados! Before anyone had a chance to react, they were swept up into the air. "Hold on, we're going for a ride!" Wonder Woman shouted.

The twister left the super heroes tumbling around, hitting each other while upside down, sideways, and backward. "Frost!" Wonder Woman yelled. "Can you freeze the tornados?"

"Yes," Frost yelled back, "but we're not allowed to use powers, only jumping!"

"That's when we're on the ground," Wonder Woman said. "Right now we're swirling in the air."

"Got it!" Frost said, and suddenly the twister froze in midair.

"Katana!" Wonder Woman called out. "Break it!"

With a couple of swift two-legged kicks from inside the burlap bag, Katana shattered the frozen twister. Team Super Hero High fell to the ground and hopped to the finish line as two members of CAD Academy, and all four students from Interstellar Magnet, tumbled off the edge of cliff, embarrassing and disqualifying themselves.

CHAPTER 28

The A/P test continued with a killer game of dodgeball—only, instead of regular balls, they used an assortment of ancient cannonballs. Heat Wave from CAD Academy hit Interstellar's Kanjar Ro so hard with a cannonball, Ro had to be carried out on a stretcher, and his alternate was put in the game.

During the three-legged race, where super heroes were paired up and two of their legs were tied together, the squabbling rose to epic levels as they tried to outrun a hail storm that was so massive it turned into a tsunami. All were caught up in the whirl, and when the water washed away, the Supers found themselves tied to their competitors.

Though the audience was having a great time, the finalist teams were not. Playing these innocuous human picnic games was far more difficult than they had expected. They had not been prepared for the water balloon toss, with balloons filled with venomous robotic lake lizards.

"In this final A/P test of the final games, the scores are as follows," the Unseen Announcer said. "In first place by only a fraction of a point is CAD Academy. At a very close second is Super Hero High, and in a distant third is Interstellar Academy. For the Triathlete of the Year, in third place is Magpie; in second place is her CAD Academy teammate Captain Cold; and leading by a wide margin, from Super Hero High, is Wonder Woman!"

Pride washed over Wonder Woman as she saw her mom cheering. She wanted to bring home the gold medal so badly. It was what she had been training for.

On the sidelines, Bumblebee sent her a hug, and Hawkgirl waved, calling, "You can do it! Go, Team Super Hero High!"

During all the weeks of training, the 24/7 of drills and studying and pushing themselves to the limit, Hawkgirl had been right there with them. Wonder Woman watched Hawkgirl, who was now blowing a kiss to her *abuela*.

"In this game," the Unseen Announcer was saying, "everyone will be given an ordinary spoon and an egg." But Wonder Woman wasn't listening. Instead, she was thinking about how proud she had made her mother, and how just being on the team was an achievement she would never forget.

The crowd cheered loudly as the announcer said, "Competitors, take your places. . . ."

"Wait!" Wonder Woman called out. She grabbed her leg. "I'm hurt!"

Wildcat, Bumblebee, and Star Sapphire raced over to her.

"Where does it hurt?" Wildcat asked. The rest of the team stood stunned. The audience was silent. Hippolyta got to her feet as the rest of the audience sat frozen in their seats.

"I can't compete," Wonder Woman told Wildcat. She had played long and hard, and had garnered most of the audience's applause. Now it was time for someone else to shine. "Put Hawkgirl in."

Wildcat looked her straight in the eyes. "Is this what you really want, Wonder Woman?" he asked evenly.

Without blinking, she answered, "This is what I want."

"You know that all you have to do is ace this last test, and no matter how the team does, you will be Super Triathlete of the Year," he reminded her.

"This is what I want," Wonder Woman repeated.

Wildcat nodded. "Okay, then," he said. "Hawkgirl, you're in!"

Bumblebee made sure Hawkgirl's Nth Metal belt and wings were in working order before sending her out. In the spoon and egg race, competitors had to weave through an obstacle course while carrying a spoon in their mouths, balancing an egg on it. In this last event of the last test, it was all powers, all weapons, anything goes.

Wonder Woman would have loved to be in the race. While some of the other challenges had been tightly monitored, this one was a free-for-all, and everyone would be going all out. Wonder Woman knew it would be the culmination of all she had learned at Super Hero High, and that she could nail it. However, in her heart, she felt that this was Hawkgirl's chance to show herself, and her grandmother, what she was made of.

As Wonder Woman sat on the sidelines, she was confident that her team would do well without her. They were that good. For a brief moment, when it was announced that the eggs housed villainous birds of prey that instantly hatched at the slightest crack, Wonder Woman sat up in anticipation. This was a challenge she had never faced before. She hoped Hawkgirl was up for the battle.

As the game began, the teams were cautious, careful not to let the eggs slip from the spoon. Still, they jostled one another and were soon flying and racing and running, using their powers and skills to throw their opponents off. It was Captain Cold who first threw his egg, knowing it would explode into an evil bird of prey, but Hawkgirl was ready for him. When the egg hit her and the bird appeared, she grabbed the bird and flew skyward, all without dropping her own egg.

Wonder Woman leaned back and watched with satisfaction. But now she was not facing the games. Knowing that Hawkgirl had everything under control, Wonder Woman was facing the stands and basking in the pride and happiness on Hawkgirl's grandmother's face as her only grandchild competed in hopes of bringing glory to Super Hero High.

Wonder Woman caught her mother's eye. Hippolyta looked solemn, and for a moment, Wonder Woman was scared. Had she let her down? Then her mother gave her a barely perceptible nod, and Wonder Woman knew that she had done the right thing. She might not win Super Triathlete of the Year—not officially—but what she had just gotten was far more valuable.

In the end, Interstellar Magnet took home the third-place trophy. There was only one point separating Super Hero High and CAD Academy for the championship, with Super Hero High coming home the victor. As the team accepted their trophy, the audience gave them a rousing standing and flying ovation. Team Super Hero High held their hands together and bowed deeply in appreciation for everything they had earned that day. But perhaps no one felt more like a winner than Wonder Woman.

Later, she congratulated Magpie, who was named Triathlete of the Year. But she and the rest of the CAD Academy team looked at Wonder Woman with disdain.

"The championship should have been ours," Captain Cold said, making it sound like a threat.

"Maybe next year," Wonder Woman said brightly. "Congratulations on your second-place win."

"Live evil," Captain Cold said bitterly to Wonder Woman. "Live evil!"

"No, thank you," Wonder Woman replied.

Back in the locker room, the team was celebrating. Everyone looked thrilled, except Golden Glider, who appeared to have a stomachache.

"Look!" Katana cried triumphantly. She was holding up her sword. "This was hidden behind some of the towel bins. That Cheetah," she said, gripping her sword even tighter. "I'll get even with her!"

Wonder Woman watched as Katana brandished her sword and sliced the air, barely missing Golden Glider. That was when she saw it. "It wasn't Cheetah," Wonder Woman gasped. "She didn't do it. Golden Glider, may I have a word with you, please?"

"What?" Golden Glider said, barely looking at her.

"Why did you do it?"

"Do what?"

"You know what I'm talking about," Wonder Woman said. "The threatening notes. Exchanging Katana's sword with an inferior one. Stealing my lasso. Trying to bring down the team."

Golden Glider yawned and picked a piece of lint off her T-shirt.

"Live evil," Wonder Woman said evenly. Golden Glider looked up, startled. "Your shirt says 'live,'" Wonder Woman pointed out. "You wore a headband that said it, too."

"So?" Golden Glider replied, looking uncomfortable.

"In the reflection of Katana's sword, the word 'live' looks like 'evil.' 'Live evil' is the unofficial motto of CAD Academy. Your brother goes there, doesn't he?"

"Maybe," Golden Glider said.

"That's right," Wonder Woman nodded. She now realized why Captain Cold had seemed so familiar. He had the same ice-blue eyes as Golden Glider—and the same arrogant attitude. "You thought that by sabotaging our team, his would win. But what I don't understand is why you would do that to your own school."

"Leave me alone," Golden Glider said. "You have no proof."

Wonder Woman reached for her Lasso of Truth. "I'm sorry," she said, "but I need to know."

Golden Glider seemed surprised to find the lasso around her wrist. Instead of looking aloof, she looked sad. "Everything in my family is about my brother, Captain Cold. I thought that if I could help his team win, my family would be proud of me," she confessed. "When you first came to our school, I knew you'd be on the team. Everyone knew that. If I could have gotten you to quit and go home, CAD Academy wouldn't have had any competition. And I'd be a hero in my house right now."

"There are better ways to be a hero," Wonder Woman told her as she took her lasso back.

Golden Glider lowered her head. "Are you going to tell Wildcat?" she asked.

"No, you are," Wonder Woman said. "You tell him that you made a mistake, and I won't tell him or Principal Waller about the threats and notes you sent me."

Golden Glider nodded.

"Now there's someone else I need to talk to," Wonder Woman said.

Cheetah was sitting with Wildcat in the empty LexCorp Arena. As Wonder Woman approached them, Wildcat stood up and patted Cheetah on the back. "Good work," he said.

Wonder Woman was confused. Maybe Wildcat wasn't as smart as she thought he was. She sat next to Cheetah. They watched the massive cleaning crew sweep up the debris before Wonder Woman spoke up.

"So you were in this with Golden Glider," she said. "I never meant to hurt you. I'm sorry you didn't make the team, but to think that you could be angry enough to do this . . . Do you hate me that much, to want to see the team fail? To see *me* fail?"

Cheetah let out a long laugh. "I'm the reason you're on the team," she said. Wonder Woman looked confused. "Who do you think nominated you? Who do you think was on the student committee that helped pick the team?"

"You?" Wonder Woman said, surprised.

"Yes, me," Cheetah said. "As much as I may dislike you, I dislike losing even more. I knew that without me, you were the best chance Team Super Hero High had of winning the championship."

"But my lasso . . . ?"

"Yeah, well. Waller suspected there was someone at school who was spying for CAD Academy and wanted to throw the games. But we didn't know who it was. Wildcat and Waller approached me and asked me to keep my eyes and ears open, and to monitor the team for any strange goings-on. That's why I was always around. I wasn't stealing your lasso; I was returning it!"

Wonder Woman felt a pain in her heart. "I am so sorry I misjudged you, Cheetah," she said. "How can I ever make it up to you?"

A sly smile stretched across Cheetah's face as she purred, "I'll think of something, Wonder Woman. You owe me big-time, and if you don't think I'll collect, you're wrong. Because one day I will. That's a promise."

CHAPTER 29

Nothing was the same for Wonder Woman after that. But then, when is any day the same as the day before? Friends and enemies and the somethings-in-between were sorted out. At least for the moment.

That morning, there were thousands of comments on Harley's HQTV site about Wonder Woman and the team. Lois Lane had written an extensive article for *Super News* and the *Daily Planet*. But what Wonder Woman was most interested in was an email she had received.

Dear Wondy,

I am so proud of you. You followed your dream and competed with your heart as the whole world watched. The fact that you helped lead your team to victory was the icing on the cake.

I loved meeting you. I'll never be a super hero, but I am dedicated to following my dream and being the best

person and musician I can be. I am honored to be your
friend.

> *Love,*
> *Mandy "Virtuoso" Bowin*

When Wonder Woman walked into the dining hall for breakfast, everyone stood and applauded. Well, not everyone. Golden Glider had been expelled. And unlike Virtuoso, who had yelled, "I'll be back!" Golden Glider silently skated away from Super Hero High and toward CAD Academy.

As the applause reached a crescendo, Wonder Woman waved and then called her teammates to her, and together they stood tall—until Beast Boy transformed into a unicorn and began running around the room. On that day, he wasn't reprimanded.

"Wondy!" Hawkgirl said, embracing her. "My *abuela* was so thrilled that she was able to see me compete in the Super Triathlon! She said it was the highlight of her life."

Both girls jumped up and down before Hawkgirl composed herself. Wonder Woman kept leaping up and down, though, thrilled to have helped make that possible for her friend.

"Wonder Woman! A word with you, please."

It was Principal Waller.

"Yes?" Wonder Woman said brightly.

Waller cleared her throat. "How's your leg?" she asked, raising one eyebrow.

"My leg? It's fine, why?" Wonder Woman asked.

"Because you were too injured to compete yesterday, and Hawkgirl had to go in to replace you?" The Wall reminded her.

Wonder Woman could feel herself turning red. "Am I in trouble?" she asked.

"You'll just have to wait and see," Principal Waller told her.

After The Wall left, Wonder Woman stood in the middle of the dining hall. She was surrounded by Supers but felt all alone. At one table were Katana, Hawkgirl, Poison Ivy, and Bumblebee, all laughing together. At another table, Green Lantern, Cyborg, The Flash, and the Riddler egged Beast Boy on to change into a chicken. Over to the left, Cheetah and Frost had their heads together, whispering while Star Sapphire filed her nails. Harley was videotaping it all.

Wonder Woman loved these people. Super Hero High was home.

The monthly assembly was sure to be boisterous. After all, Super Hero High had brought home the trophy for the one hundredth Super Triathlon. As Principal Waller spoke, the teachers sat behind her on their thrones, glowing as if they each were the winner themselves. And in part, they were. The students in the audience were just as excited. To go to a school that made history was something to be proud of.

"Thank you, Team Super Hero High!" Principal Waller said as the team returned to their seats. "And now I have another announcement. This month's Hero of the Month."

It took a while for everyone, teachers included, to calm down. Principal Waller waited. What she had to say next could not be rushed.

"Super Hero High's next Hero of the Month is . . ."

Wonder Woman looked around. Who could it be? Not her. Not after Waller had discovered she'd faked her injury.

"WONDER WOMAN!" Principal Waller announced.

Huh?

"Wonder Woman, please come back onstage and join me."

Bumblebee pushed her toward the stage as everyone cheered. "Go!" she whispered.

What?

Wonder Woman stood stunned as she listened to Principal Waller. "This month's Super Hero has brought pride and dedication to our school. She has proved herself to be a leader, and, even more rare, a selfless one. Putting others before herself. She is not here for personal glory, but for the greater good, and to shine the spotlight on others. That is what a true leader does." Wonder Woman thought she saw the principal wink at her.

As the video played, Wonder Woman choked back tears. Her fellow students and teachers all talked about how much they admired her. Even Cheetah said, "I don't want to like her, but sometimes I think I do. Wait! Did I just say that?"

When the lights came back on, Principal Waller continued. "And now, Wonder Woman, as your first assignment as Hero of the Month, you will be showing our newest Super Hero High student around the school. Oh! Here she comes now!"

The entire auditorium, including Wonder Woman, looked to the back of the room. A girl with long blond hair, a battered suitcase, and a huge smile was flying toward the stage. But instead of stopping, she mowed down several teachers before crashing into the wall and falling face-first on the ground.

Undeterred, she jumped up and smoothed the front of her red skirt, dusted some dirt off her short cape—a *short* cape! what a genius idea—and then ran over to Wonder Woman, tripping twice, but jumping up each time as if nothing had happened. Her eyes bright, she held out her hand.

"I am a huge, huge, huge fan!" the girl gushed. "I am *sooooo* excited to meet you, Wonder Woman. I hope we can be friends! Can we? Please say yes!"

"Yes, of course," Wonder Woman said, smiling. "And what is your name?"

"Oh, oops!" The girl's blue eyes sparkled as she laughed. "Of course I should introduce myself . . . my name is Supergirl!"

To be continued. . . .

Lisa Yee's debut novel, *Millicent Min, Girl Genius,* won the prestigious Sid Fleischman Humor Award. With nearly two million books in print, her other novels for young readers include *Stanford Wong Flunks Big-Time*; *Absolutely Maybe; Bobby vs. Girls (Accidentally)*; *Bobby the Brave (Sometimes)*; *Warp Speed; The Kidney Hypothetical, Or How to Ruin Your Life in Seven Days*; and American Girl's Kanani books, *Good Luck, Ivy,* and the 2016 Girl of the Year books. Lisa has been a Thurber House Children's Writer-in-Residence, and her books have been named an NPR Best Summer Read, a *Sports Illustrated* Kids Hot Summer Read, and a *USA Today* Critics' Pick, among other accolades. Visit Lisa at LisaYee.com.